WITCHFUL THINKING

A Cozy Paranormal Mystery

KRISTEN PAINTER

Welcome to Everlasting

Want to know when Kristen's next book is coming out?
Join her mailing list for release news, fun giveaways, insider scoop and more! NEWSLETTER.

The Happily Everlasting Series

COZY PARANORMAL MYSTERY ROMANCE NOVELS

Dead Man Talking
by Jana DeLeon

Once Hunted, Twice Shy
by Mandy M. Roth

Fooled Around and Spelled in Love
by Michelle M. Pillow

Witchful Thinking
by Kristen Painter

Visit Everlasting
https://welcometoeverlasting.com/

About Witchful Thinking

A HAPPILY EVERLASTING SERIES NOVEL

Welcome to Everlasting, Maine, where there's no such thing as normal.

Charlotte Fenchurch knows that, which is why she's not that surprised when a very special book of magic falls into her hands at the library where she works. As a fledgling witch, owning her own grimoire is a dream come true. But there's something…mysterious about the book she just can't figure out.

Leopard shifter Walker Black knows what's odd about the book. It's full of black magic and so dangerous that it could destroy the world. Good thing the Fraternal Order of Light has sent him to Everlasting to recover it and put it into safe storage. If he has to, he'll even take the witch who owns it into custody.

That is until he meets Charlotte and realizes she's not out to watch the world burn. She's sweet and kind and wonderful. Suddenly protecting her is all he wants to do. Well, that and kiss her some more. But dark forces seem determined to get their hands on the book, making Charlotte their target, and Walker worries that he won't be able to protect her from them – or the organization he works for.

Can Walker and Charlotte survive the onslaught of danger? Or is that just witchful thinking?

To Mandy M. Roth, Michelle M. Pillow, and Jana DeLeon - thanks for being crazier than I am and actually making this thing happen. Y'all are a special kind of magic.

Chapter One

Charlotte Fenchurch stared down at the library cart of books waiting to be reshelved and wished for the hundredth time in as many days that her recently acquired status as a witch also came with immediate powers.

It did not, and while she was learning new spells and bettering her existing skills every day, nothing she knew so far would allow her to instantly put all of these books back into place with the twitch of her nose like certain classic television programs would have one believe.

Sadly, she had also been informed by her mentor and most powerful witch extraordinaire, Lola Honeycutt, that nose twitching *only* worked on television. Be that as it may, Charlotte had discovered that she could levitate books and place them into their appropriate spots if she concentrated and only did one book at a time.

This wasn't a skill, however, that could be utilized when the library had patrons in it. Or when her boss and head librarian, Mildred Merriweather, was around. (The same went for Norm Poole, the part-time librarian.) Neither Millie nor Norm were witches, and coven rules specifically stated that spells were not to be demonstrated within viewing range of ordinaries. In other words, non-witchy human types.

And while Everlasting was a curious town filled with interestingly gifted people and quite a few citizens who believed in things that went bump in the night, it also had its share of regular, non-magical folks.

Resigned to doing things the ordinary way, Charlotte started sorting the books in order of how they needed to be reshelved. General References was first. But that book was old, and the musty smell of it made Charlotte's nose itch with an impending sneeze.

She went to the front desk to grab a tissue and found Millie with another old book in her hands. Charlotte helped herself to a tissue from the box on the desk.

Millie gave Charlotte some side eye as if to say nose blowing was time wasting, then let out a heavy, perturbed sigh.

Charlotte glanced at her boss as she finished blowing her nose. Millie's hair, a gray helmet of precise curls, looked especially helmet-y today. Charlotte sniffed once more for good measure and was about to comment that sometimes noses had to be blown, when Millie's frown deepened dramatically.

"This is *not* a library book." Millie shook her head. Not a hair moved. That hair, combined with her tall, slender frame, often made Charlotte think her boss looked like a steel Q-tip. Not the most flattering of descriptions, perhaps, but one that fit.

Although a grumpy steel Q-tip would have been even more perfect, because it wasn't so unusual for Millie to be bothered by something.

Millie ran a tight ship. So tight that it was a wonder she didn't squeak when she walked. Norm, the part-time librarian, had actually said that once. Not in front of Millie, obviously. Millie would have reprimanded him on the spot, then probably added a note in his file. She held little truck with rule breakers, scofflaws, and those she considered slackers. (Which included a shockingly high percentage of the townspeople.)

Someone had apparently violated one of her set-in-stone rules. Namely the one about putting donated books into the returned book drop box. Mixing the two was a big no-no in Millie's world.

The offending object was still in Millie's gaunt

hands, a shabby thing about the size of a dictionary with a tattered leather cover and gilded pages that had long since lost their golden gleam. Shame. Charlotte loved books in any condition, but this one had not been well-cared for. "Maybe it could be restored—"

"No." Millie clucked her tongue and shook her head as she pulled the book away from Charlotte's gaze. "This book should have been discarded, not donated. The title is completely worn off."

Pain clenched Charlotte's heart a little. The thought of a book being discarded had that effect on her. Books were…well, everything.

Millie tried to open the book and snorted. "And the pages have been glued together. Abominable." She tossed the book into the trash bin.

The heavy clunk of it dropping to the bottom pealed like a death knell through Charlotte's soul as she went back to her cart of books. Even if the pages had been glued together, it could still be decorative. Books always looked nice on a shelf. Or under a plant. No book deserved such an inglorious end as the trash bin.

A boisterous laugh cut through the library's reverent stillness. Sounded like Bobby Driscoll. He was a slightly wild young man who'd had the misfortune of being born into one of the wealthiest families in Everlasting, meaning he'd also had the misfortune of being coddled and allowed to get away with his generally bad behavior.

Millie's head jerked up at the sound. Loud noises were not permitted while she was on duty. Like a dog on the scent of a steak she left the pile of returned books behind and stalked off toward the Natural Sciences section to reprimand whoever had dared to find something funny among those volumes of information.

Charlotte left the cart behind once again, made a bee-line for the trash and rescued the book. She held it down low so that if Millie looked over, she wouldn't see that Charlotte had pulled it out of the bin.

Charlotte glanced at the cover. Definitely leather. It was warm in her hands. And not nearly in as bad of shape as it had seemed. The gold-leafed title was flaking off in a few spots, but she had no problem reading the words. *Middian's Book of Curiosities, Curses, & Commanding Hexes*. Understanding those words wasn't hard either. Especially the curses and hexes part. As a fledging witch, she knew what those were. She couldn't cast any, but she got the general idea. Curses and hexes were generally considered dark magic, which wasn't something the witches in the Everlasting coven ever dabbled in. Sure, there were other witches in town who approached magic differently, and had no intentions of joining the coven, but they were all good witches that she knew of. Not at all the sort to use dark magic either.

Charlotte liked the coven's approach, though. She'd been told that when she became a full-fledged witch and was sworn in, she'd have to pledge herself to all that was good and right. Something she'd do happily and without hesitation.

That didn't stop her from being interested in the book, however. There could still be something to learn from it. Maybe she'd take it with her to the next meeting and—

"Hello there, Miss Fenchurch."

She glanced up at the familiar, wispy voice and smiled. "Hello, Judge Turnbury. You're late today. I was getting worried about you."

"Arthritis slows me down sometimes, but I wouldn't miss a day." He shuffled on by, today's newspaper tucked under his arm. He'd be nodding off in the reading room in under twenty minutes if today followed his normal routine. Which it most likely would. Gilbert Turnbury had been a judge in Everlasting until his retirement ten years ago. His wife had passed on not long after that, leaving him alone. It was no secret how much he missed her. He'd started coming to the library for the grief support meetings.

The library was so many things to so many people. Just one of the reasons she loved being a librarian.

But the biggest reason was in her hand. She went back to the book. She *had* to take this book home. She almost felt compelled. Like it was… meant for her. She started to lift the book for a better inspection.

"Can you tell me where the sci-fi books are?"

She tucked the book under the counter and looked up. Into the most serene green-gold eyes she'd ever seen. The rest of this man, however, looked positively devilish. Black hair a little too long, strong brows, and the shadow of stubble accented his squared jaw. Throw in his black leather jacket and the dark sunglasses pushed up onto this head and he was clearly doused in trouble.

This wasn't really the first time Charlotte had seen him, though. Just the first time she'd seen him this close. The man had been coming into the library for the past week, but he'd yet to check anything out.

She pointed toward the stacks he'd asked about. "On the other side of romance."

He laughed, and the sound sent a lick of plea-sure down her spine, confirming his devilishness. A man's laugh should not have that effect on a woman's sensibilities.

"What's on *this* side of romance?" he asked.

She stared at him, at a loss for words. She wasn't a sparkling conversationalist, she knew that. She was a woman who preferred animals and books over most people. But she could usually come up with something. Just not, apparently, when faced with this bastion of male temptation.

He stuck his hand out. The inside of his wrist bore a Mobius strip tattoo. "Walker Black. I'm new in town."

"Walker?" Most of the men she knew were Jim or Bill or Mike. This was Maine, after all. The land of frugal living and practical values. And Walker seemed neither a frugal nor a practical first name. "That's quite a moniker."

He grinned. "It's a family name."

She was still staring. It was hard not to. His smile almost sparkled. She blinked herself out of his spell and shook his hand, trying to make as little actual contact as possible. Hard to do in a hand-shake. His grip was firm and warm and made her want to hold on longer than was polite. Definitely trouble. "Welcome to Everlasting."

Ooo, there was a dazzling bit of conversation. She almost rolled her eyes at herself.

"Thanks…" He squinted at her name tag. "Charlotte. Nice name. Do you ever go by Charlie?"

"No." That was a boy's name. And while she might not be the girliest girl to ever live in this town, she certainly didn't want to be called by a boy's name.

"Good," he said, surprising her. "Charlotte suits you."

"I suppose you're here for the Cranberry Festival?" The month-long extravaganza brought a lot of business—and tourists—to town. The place was crawling with them, but the library was rarely on their list of must-see places.

"Something like that." His gaze swept over her like he was in charge of doing a Charlotte Fenchurch inventory. The nerve. "I'm going to need a library card, too. Can you help me with that?"

"Yes." That much she could do. She got out the form and presented it to him with a pen. "You'll need to fill this out. Also, for a non-resident card, there's a twenty-five-dollar fee. The card is only good for one month. Unless you want to pay for a whole year. That's two hundred and ninety dollars. And you can only take out one book at a time."

He gave her a slightly surprised look. "Not a fan of the tourists, huh?"

"The tourists are fine. We just don't want them leaving with our books."

"Good to know. And one month will do me just fine." He read over the form she'd given him, then took the pen and started scratching away. "I don't usually give out my number to women I've just met."

Was he flirting with her? The mischievous sparkle in his eyes said he was. Men didn't generally flirt with Charlotte. Not men who looked like this. Not that Skip Hartman, the teller at the bank who always gave her a lollipop, even though technically those were for kids, was unattractive. He was nice enough looking. (And seemed on the verge of asking her out.) But he wasn't the kind of handsome that made you forget to breathe.

Like the man in front of her.

Whatever Mr. Black's game was, she wasn't falling for it. She knew her shortcomings far too well to think that this decadent example of the male species was remotely interested in her. Her medium brown hair and regular brown (hazel on a good day) eyes didn't inspire flirting. "Don't worry, I'll only use it if you have an overdue book."

He seemed to consider that. "How long before a book is overdue?"

"Two weeks."

He sighed. "Seems a helluva long time to wait, but all right." Before she could say anything else, he bent his head and went back to filling out the form. The tip of his tongue stuck out from between his perfect white teeth.

It was such an innocent expression, she instantly wondered if she'd misjudged him. "I'll be right back."

"Mm-hmm," he muttered.

She slipped the book she'd rescued from the trash from under the counter and, holding it down low, spirited it away to the breakroom and into her big tote bag, which she then stuffed back into her labeled cubby. With the book safely secured, she went back to the counter.

Mr. Black was done with his form and was once again smiling at her. "Here you go." He slid the paper and twenty-five dollars in cash toward her.

She processed his library card as quickly as she could, then pointed him in the direction of the sci-fi books again. Millie returned as he was walking away, so Charlotte tucked the money into the cash drawer and went back to her cart. "I'm going to reshelve these."

Millie gave her a strange look. "You don't need to tell me you're going to do your job, Miss Fenchurch. Just do it."

"Yes, ma'am." This was another of those times that Charlotte wished she wasn't just a fledging witch and had the ability to put a frog in Millie's lunch or give the woman a strange, unexplainable rash. But as Lola had repeatedly told her, witchcraft should only be used for good or one would suffer the blowback of karma.

So no frogs or rashes, but there had to be something Charlotte could do to mellow Millie out. She considered what sort of simple spell she could cast. She'd done well with the levitation ones, but she didn't see how lifting Millie into the air would do anything but freak her out.

The *ustulo* command was the one Charlotte really need to practice. Especially with Lola due back from giving one of her lectures and doing a book signing in Boston. Charlotte wanted her mentor to know she'd used her time wisely. And Lola had told her *ustulo* was one of the most basic spells there was, useful for lighting candles and starting fires in fireplaces, that sort of thing. All Charlotte had managed to do with it so far was nearly set her apartment on fire and turn one very expensive Yankee Candle into a jar of boiling wax. But that's why she needed to practice. Now, what kind of candle might she light this evening on Millie's behalf?

Charlotte pushed her cart into the stacks as she gave that some thought. Maybe the woman needed a love spell cast on her. Then she'd have someone else to focus on. Or *maybe* being in love, if that was possible for an uptight woman like Millie, might soften her up. Millie had been married once upon a time, so clearly it was possible for her to fall in love. Now who should she direct that spell's intent toward? Judge Turnbury? He could use a woman in his life. It might even take his mind off his late wife.

But Millie might be more a curse than a blessing. Charlotte snorted out loud at the very idea.

"Something funny?"

She jumped and turned to see Mr. Black behind her. "You're still here?"

He leaned against the stack. "Is there a time

limit on how long someone's allowed to stay in the library?"

"No, but…" She glanced at the clock on the wall behind him. "You've been here for half an hour."

"I'm still looking for something to read."

"I thought you wanted a sci-fi. This isn't the science-fiction section." Her words came out crosser than she'd intended, but she wasn't a fan of being surprised. Hated it, actually. How anyone watched a scary movie was beyond her.

"Nope, it isn't. I moved on. Sorry about startling you."

"Yes, well, I'm fine. Thank you. So you want something from the metaphysical section?"

He shrugged. "I like to read all sorts of things." He gave her that look again, like he was sizing her up. "What do you like to read?"

Books were the way to her heart. But she doubted he knew that. He was just making conversation. "I'll read pretty much anything. Thrillers, biographies, cookbooks—not that I'm a great chef —foreign language translations—"

"What are you reading now?"

She hesitated, not because she was ashamed of her current selection but because technically she wasn't reading it, she was rereading it. "A book I've read many times before. *The Scoundrel Prince*."

"Never heard of it."

"Doesn't surprise me. It's a romance. A historical romance, to boot." She made a face at him. "I'm sure you wouldn't like it."

He crossed his arms. The sleeves of his jacket stretched tight over his biceps, and for a split second she wondered what he looked like shirtless. "Oh really? Why? Because I'm a guy? Isn't that a little judgmental?"

It was. But it was also based on years of experience and a keen understanding of what men typically liked to read. "So you're interested in it, then?"

"Absolutely. Hook me up."

She studied him for a moment. There was no mockery in his eyes, nothing flippant about his smile or his tone of voice. "Okay, follow me."

She took him to the romance section and found the book easily. She knew exactly where it was because she recommended it quite often and the library had two copies. One of which had been checked out three days ago by Helena Grimaldi, who also reread the book at least once a year, but the other was in its place on the shelf.

She pulled it down and handed it to him. "There you go."

She watched his face as he took in the cover with its passionately embracing couple replete in their slightly historically inaccurate outfit of breeches on him and a flowing, but nearly falling off, ball gown on her.

Mr. Black looked up at her. "How about when I'm done with this, we discuss it over dinner?"

Charlotte's brows lifted. "That implies you'll actually read it, Mr. Black."

"I plan to. And call me Walker, please. Dinner, then?"

"I don't know…" Dinner was a big commitment for someone whose last date had involved going with a second cousin to a third cousin's wedding.

"Lunch?"

"Hard to do when I'm here. I only get half an hour."

"Coffee, then. With nothing planned afterward."

"I suppose that would be all right." Especially because she doubted he'd finish the book. And if he lied about it, she'd know. She knew the book backward and forward. Just like she knew that Mr. Black —Walker was up to something. Which was almost forgivable given how he looked like he could be on the cover of a romance novel himself. She could just about picture him in a pirate's shirt, sword on his hip, hair blowing in the brisk, sea breeze.

"Great. Coffee it is, then." He tipped his head. "Check me out?"

"What?" She snapped out of her reverie, unaware she'd been so obvious.

He waggled the book. "Can you check this book out for me?"

"Oh, yes, sure."

They went back to the desk, and she got him sorted as quickly as possible. Millie was at the desk too, working on the computer. Probably compiling the next list of late notices to go out. Or tallying fines.

Charlotte watched Walker leave. He'd better not abscond with that copy of *The Scoundrel Prince*.

"Miss Fenchurch, you may take your break now."

"Hmm?" Charlotte looked at Millie, then checked the time. Lunch break already. But her appetite was for something much different than the chicken salad sandwich awaiting her. Much different. And much more appealing.

Chapter Two

Walker climbed into his truck in the library's parking lot. Today's visit hadn't been as fruitful as he would have liked, but it was still a better day than he'd had after a week here. He'd made contact at least, and it had gone reasonably well. That's how cases went sometimes. Some started slow and some started with gunfire. Literally.

But he had yet to pinpoint the cause of the bitter aroma that accompanied all dark magic. The odor had been present in the library since he'd started coming. At first, he'd assumed it was a clue the book had arrived. Now, he wasn't so sure the scent wasn't a sign that the Collective's agent had been there. Or was still there.

It could also be that there was a witch with bad intentions in the building.

He zipped his leather jacket, then stuffed the

KRISTEN PAINTER

romance novel inside for safe keeping before starting up the vehicle. Charlotte Fenchurch was most definitely a witch, and a very cute one on top of that, but there was no indication that she was *that* witch. Or that the book he was after was anywhere on the shelves. He'd been up and down the rows every day he'd been in the library, and his sixth sense for the presence of magic hadn't narrowed in on anything.

Except for when he'd been around Charlotte, which was how he knew what she was. Well, that and the information the FOL had supplied him.

Didn't mean the book wasn't in the library. He was pretty sure it was. Again, based on the FOL intel. What it most likely meant was that the book just hadn't found its way to a shelf yet. It could also mean Charlotte already had possession of it. Fortunately, the romance novel tucked into his jacket gave him a new excuse to return to the library and a reason to see her again. He'd go further in that direction before breaking into her home to make sure she hadn't already taken the book there.

He shifted into drive and headed for the apartment he was renting near the waterfront. It was the attic of a three-story Victorian that had once been a stately mansion but was now divided into apartments of various sizes.

The apartment in the Marlboro House was paid through the month and larger than he needed, but it suited him well. He would only be in Everlasting until he found the book, and he didn't always keep regular hours. The apartment had dormer windows he could slip in and out of, plus the building's exterior had a lot of trims, moldings, and balconies to make the climb up or down an easy one. Although stairs were his first choice, in his line of work, being able to come and go with some stealth was sometimes a necessary thing.

His line of work being an agent for the Fraternal Order of Light. And as an FOL agent, his job was the recovery of dangerous and occasionally deadly magical objects. In this case, that object was the rare copy of Middian's that had found its way home to the small fishing village of Everlasting, Maine.

The book wasn't just rare and dangerous, it was extremely dangerous. In the wrong hands, Middian's could end the world. Granted, the person would have to be highly skilled and bent on destruction, and Charlotte didn't come off like someone out to watch the world burn, but he'd seen enough craziness to know that no one should be underestimated.

Just like this town. It seemed like a sleepy fishing village that got a little economical boost from the occasional influx of tourists looking to gorge themselves on lobster rolls, but there was something else going on here. And he wasn't just thinking about the Cranberry Festival (which was causing more than the average bump in tourists). There was something just beneath the surface. He wasn't sure what it was yet, but the thrum of magic was as present here as the tang of salt air and the occasional aroma of a fishing boat in need of a good hose down.

And the stench of the dark arts.

Sure, New England was nice enough, but it was a touch cool for his tastes in October. And a little too sparse. The trees were bare of their leaves except for a few crispy stragglers. It was an interesting change from his last adventure in the panhandle of Florida, but it was only going to stay interesting for so long.

He parked his truck in the lot behind the Marlboro House and headed inside. As he climbed the stairs, his phone vibrated. He took it out and checked the screen.

The Collective's agent is already there.

With a few choice expletives, Walker ran the rest of the steps. He let himself into his room, locking the door behind him, then called his supervisor, Clark Stillwell. Probably not his real name. Or at least not the one he'd been born with.

"Black checking in. Got the text. Any idea where their agent is?"

"No." Stillwell was a man of few words. "You went to the library?"

"Yes. No sign of the book yet, but it has to be there by now. Based on the smell of dark magic, I'd say it definitely is. Plus, Flora's been dead a week and a half. That's enough time."

"Has been in the past."

Flora Mae Wellington, the previous owner of Middian's, had died at the ripe old age of eighty-seven and three quarters. Not bad for a witch who, despite her sweet old lady name, specialized in the dark arts. Practicing black magic tended to take a toll on a person, and Flora had been menacing the unsuspecting people of Oklahoma City since her thirties, when she'd moved there.

From Everlasting.

The book, which apparently considered this quaint little village its home, specifically the town's library, always returned here when its current owner passed on. The file Walker had been given said Flora had gotten the book the summer before she'd moved to Oklahoma. In theory, to be closer to her widowed sister. But maybe it was her way of getting out of town after she'd found the book in the stacks of the Everlasting library.

Not that it was all as cut and dried as it sounded.

The book didn't respond to everyone. Grimoires, or books of magic, could be fickle like that, and Middian's was no exception. In fact, very few people could even open it. To those who couldn't because they lacked the special witchy abilities necessary, the book appeared old and worn with no discernable title. It was often thrown away. That didn't seem to hurt the book in any way, because no matter what happened to it, the book always showed up on a shelf somewhere in the library and sat there until it was discovered by its new owner, however long that might take.

But for those who had the right magical gifts, the book appeared very differently. Its title was plainly readable, as were the pages inside. And that's when things got tricky.

Because not only did the pages hold incredibly powerful and dangerous spells for the right people, but when that right person opened the book after bonding with it, the opener was granted one wish at any point in their lifetime.

Flora Mae had used hers to get a cookie jar that was perpetually full of gold coins. Unfortunately for her heirs, the granted wish became null and void upon the death of the book's owner. The cookie jar had gone poof.

But there was no telling what the Collective, an organization of power-hungry megalomaniacs, would do with that wish. They'd been trying to get their hands on the book for a very long time. They'd had it several times throughout history, employing an array of powerful witches able to use the book at will. The last time they'd had it, they'd failed to get the wish. The witch who owned the book had used it already, but the Collective had managed to kill the FOL agent in charge of the book's recovery and subsequently blown up the Hindenburg.

There would be no disasters on Walker's watch. He'd taken an oath to serve the Fraternal Order of Light in whatever capacity necessary to accomplish his missions and he meant it. He'd grown up in the service of the FOL. He'd known no other life. No other family.

Once he had possession of the book, he'd have until midnight to put it in the specially designed case that would negate the book's magic. Then it could be safely transported to the FOL's nearest vault and secured for good. Otherwise at midnight, the book would return itself to the library.

It would always return to the library. At least until it was bonded to the witch who was meant to be its new owner. Then it would return itself to the witch that owned it, and would continue to do that until that witch passed on.

If by some chance the book had already found its new owner, Walker was going to have to take it away from that witch, something that wasn't going to be nearly as easy as strolling into the library. In fact, it might result in him bringing in the book *and* the witch.

He really hoped it didn't come to that. And he really hoped that witch wasn't Charlotte. He unzipped his jacket, took out the paperback she'd given him, and tossed it on the bed. He hung the jacket up and put his phone on the nightstand before grabbing a protein bar from his stash and settling down on the bed to plow through as many chapters of the book as possible.

This was definitely the first time a mission had required him to read a romance novel.

Focusing on the pages proved more difficult than he'd imaged, though. It wasn't because of the story, but rather the pretty witch who kept popping into his head.

What if she was the Collective's agent? She didn't seem like the type who'd be interested in world domination or evil geniuses. And he didn't really want her to be.

Because Walker wasn't just any FOL agent. He was more than that. Much more. For one thing, he was a leopard shifter. Most of the recovery agents were some kind of supernatural. It made the job easier.

But Walker was also a witch hunter, trained in the art of fighting dark magic and the devious prac-titioners of it. Witches who'd gone to the dark side were very dangerous creatures, but he'd chosen that specialty because the man who'd raised him had been an FOL witch hunter. And that skill was why he'd been sent here on this particular mission. He could sense witches. Knew how to fight them. Knew how to survive their magic. Knew how to contain it.

He had never failed a mission. He wouldn't this

time either. One way or another, no matter what obstacles fell into his path, no matter what measures he had to take, the book was coming back with him.

CHARLOTTE WAS DISTRACTED. And not just because of the smooth-talking Mr. Black. *Walker*. She snorted. Honestly, what kind of name was that? The kind of name a romance hero would have. But that was beside the point.

It was also hard not to be curious about the interesting book in her tote bag. Even more than Walker, she couldn't stop thinking about it. How had it come to be in the drop-off box? Had someone actually meant to donate it? Who had it belonged to? And why would they get rid of a book like that? It looked old. And maybe valuable. There could be a name inside. Lots of old, donated books had the owner's name scrawled on the inside cover.

"Hello, Charlotte."

"Sheriff Bull, nice to see you." Francine Bull was always on the job. Although sometimes that job was less about law enforcement and more about finding the nearest handsome man. Her cool, gray gaze scanned the library for signs of trouble (probably) even as she stood in front of Charlotte. "Arrest anyone interesting lately?"

Francine laughed and finally made eye contact.

"Not in this town. At best, I'll probably catch Owen McCreary jaywalking again."

"Not likely, as he's in the historical room working on his lecture." Owen was the head of the Everlasting Historical Society and always gave a talk at the Cranberry Festival. "Speaking of, with the Festival going on, there's always a chance for a drunk and disorderly among the tourists."

Her eyes narrowed. "Possibly. I like to make an example of the first one. Sets the tone, you know?"

"Absolutely."

She put her hand on the counter and leaned in. "You have that new Jack Reacher for me?"

"I do. Just a sec." She went back to the hold shelf and pulled the book. Sheriff Bull was always the first to get the new Jack Reacher. It's just how things worked in Everlasting. Charlotte carried it back, scanned the barcode and handed it to her. "There you go. Evelyn White's next on the list so don't dally."

"Evelyn can wait her turn. I like to savor a good book, not treat it like fast food." She rolled her eyes. "Say, anything else interesting come in? You know I'm always looking for something new and even with the savoring, this Reacher won't last me more than three days tops."

Sheriff Bull liked Lee Childs, Elmore Leonard, and Jackie Collins. Any books that were similar were fine, but rarely lived up in her estimation. Unfortunately, Childs was the only one still producing new books since he was the only living author of the three, which meant Charlotte was always on the lookout for books the sheriff might like. She thought about the book in her tote bag. "Nothing that I think would suit your tastes, but I'll keep my eyes out."

"All right, I'm off to lunch. You let me know." She touched the brim of her hat.

"Will do. Enjoy your lunch."

"Oh, I will. It's with Deputy June." Francine winked as she headed out.

Charlotte snickered. Besides the sheriff's love of a few very specific authors, she enjoyed the company of attractive young *male* police officers. So much so that attractive young police officers seemed to be about the only kind she hired. And she hired so many, they'd gotten together and released a calendar.

The project had been a hit and raised a tremendous amount for the police force. Problem was, it had been so popular, the officers had come to be known by their months more than their names. Fortunately, the guys certainly didn't mind the nicknames or the attention. (Truth be told, the calendar men had perpetuated the nicknames once they'd realized that was good for sales. And getting dates.)

In fact, the officers liked the attention so much, most of them had signed up for the bachelor auction that was a part of the Cranberry Festival. Charlotte couldn't fault them, though. Everlasting had a very healthy law enforcement budget because of it all.

Hmm. Maybe Walker was hoping to become a deputy. He'd said he was new and that he'd come for the Festival, but not how long he was staying or what his purpose at the Festival was. And he'd listed the Marlboro House as his address. She didn't think they rented to short termers. Not that she cared. At all.

But if he didn't return that copy of *The Scoundrel Prince*, she'd care. She'd care so much she'd track him down and make *him* care.

Chapter Three

Walker's phone buzzed, pulling him from the depths of *The Scoundrel Prince*. Through the dormer window in his attic apartment, a few stars were faintly visible in the darkening sky. He sat up, surprised, and checked his watch. A little after six p.m. He'd been reading since he'd gotten home from the library.

He hadn't expected that at all. Not with a romance novel. He squinted at the book, his mind drifting back to the pretty witch who'd hoisted it upon him. Could it be that she'd bespelled the book to keep him occupied? Nothing about the physical book set off his magical radar, but maybe Charlotte was more powerful than he'd guessed.

Her bewitching the book would imply that she might know something about him. Like why he was here. And what he was after. Why else would she want to keep him occupied?

It also would tip the scales in favor of her actually being a member of the Collective. Or at least working for them.

He sat up, closed the book, and put it aside. She must have done it. Why else would he have lost himself in a romance novel? He grunted in disgust. Maybe the book had been good, but he couldn't be sure now. And he'd broken one of his own rules with Charlotte. He'd underestimated her.

That caused a small fission of anger to crawl up his spine. How powerful a witch was she?

He had no choice but to find out. But he couldn't exactly come right out and ask her. Experience told him witches didn't usually respond very well to questions like that.

He tucked his phone into his pocket, then grabbed his keys and jacket, throwing the jacket on as he hustled down the stairs to his truck. He headed toward Main Street. In small towns like this, everyone knew everybody, and there were a couple of places to get the info he was looking for. One of them was the hairdresser, but he'd stick out there like a sore thumb. Then there was the local watering hole, which seemed to be a pool hall called the Magic Eight Ball, but it was a little early to be drinking and he sucked at pool. That left the third option, the diner.

That was perfect, because the protein bar he'd scarfed down hadn't done much. He was starving.

Fortunately, Everlasting's diner was right in the heart of town so he didn't have to go far. He hadn't eaten there yet, since he'd been keeping things low-key in case the Collective's agent spotted him before Walker spotted him or her.

But time was running out, and honestly, if the Collective's agent wanted to start something, Walker was game.

He parked in front of Chickadee's Diner, snagging a prime spot only because another car pulled out. He turned the engine off and looked through the windows. There was a decent crowd inside, being that he'd arrived during peak dinner hours. He went in and managed to find a free stool at the counter.

A server swung by almost immediately. Betsy, from her name tag. She looked like she'd been working at Chickadee's since it had opened, which according to the sign, was in the late '60's. Or maybe the shellacked bouffant and black, cat-eye glasses with rhinestones in the corners were just part of the uniform. "Getcha something to drink?"

"Coffee. Black."

"Comin' up."

While she got that, he checked out the menu printed on the paper place mat in front of him. Today was Wednesday, which meant the special was pot roast. Good enough.

She came back with the coffee. "Ready to order?"

"Pot roast special."

"Good choice." She scribbled his order on her notepad, then ripped the page off and stuck it under a clip on a horizontal wheel that turned between the kitchen and the front of the diner. "Order up," she yelled through the window as she spun the wheel to move the ticket to the kitchen side. That done, she was off to check on the rest of her customers.

Walker sighed. Coming in during the dinner rush wasn't the best time to engage a server in conversation, but there were always the locals. He glanced to his left.

The man was about a hundred years old and had enough stray hairs growing out of his ears to make Walker question the guy's ability to even hear a conversation.

He had better luck on his right. Two cops in uniform. Sheriff's deputies, actually. And both of them were eating the pot roast special. He nodded a greeting. "Evening, officers."

They nodded back.

"How's tonight's special? I've never eaten here before."

They laughed. The one closest to him lifted a forkful of mashed potatoes dripping in gravy.

"You're gonna like it unless you don't like diner food, and then I don't know what you're doing eating here in the first place."

"I love diner food. Happy to hear it's a good choice. I'm new to town, so trying to figure out the best spots, where the locals go, that sort of thing."

The second man leaned forward to see Walker better. "You're at one of the local spots right now. Lot of tourists in town with the Festival, though, so it might be hard to tell."

"Good to know. What else is worth eating here?"

"All of it," the first officer said. "But make sure you get a slice of the blueberry crumble. Best you'll ever have. The cranberry apple pie is good too."

Betsy returned to refill Walker's coffee as the officer was speaking. His words broke her out into a big smile. "That's right, the blueberry crumble is the pie to have." She eyed Walker. "You want me to save you one? Doesn't always last through the dinner rush."

He put on his best charming smile. "I don't think I could eat a whole pie."

He got the result he wanted when she laughed. "How about just a slice, then?"

"Perfect. Thank you, Betsy. I'm Walker."

"Nice to meet you, Walker." She popped her hip out to one side. "Lemme put your name on that slice and bring you your dinner."

A minute later he was staring down at a steaming plateful of pot roast, boiled carrots, green beans, a mountain of mashed potatoes covered in brown gravy and a fat dinner roll with two foil-wrapped pats of butter beside it.

Good thing he was hungry. This was a massive amount of food. He tucked in, swallowing his first bite before engaging the deputies again. "Oh man, you were right. This is good stuff."

"Told ya," the man next to him said.

Walker split the roll and slathered each side with butter. "I guess you guys know just about everyone in town."

The man next to him nodded. "Pretty much."

"Any chance you know Charlotte at the library?"

"Sure. Nice girl. Quiet. Kind of stereotypical librarian. Very smart. Loves books. Pretty sure she has a cat."

Most witches did. They called them familiars, and the animals helped them focus their magic. Made sense a powerful witch like Charlotte would have one. But cats were generally no big deal, seeing as how he was one himself. Not that being a leopard shifter was the same thing as being a house cat. At all.

He kept digging. "Is she seeing anyone?"

"Don't know that." The deputy looked at his partner. "You know, July?"

July (although the man's badge said Simons)

shook his head. "I don't think she is." He glanced at Walker. "You thinking about asking her out?"

"I sort of already did."

Both men smiled like they knew what he was up to.

Walker laughed. "I don't usually work that fast, but she seemed nice, and she sort of challenged me to read this book—a romance novel if you can believe that—and…" He shrugged. "We're going to talk about it over coffee after I read it."

July smirked. "Buddy, I think you got asked out, not the other way around."

Walker picked up his fork. "No way."

The other officer snorted. "She challenged you to read a romance novel, you agreed, and you think you're the one calling the shots? What kind of romance novel was it?"

Walker shook his head even as he answered. "Historical romance."

The deputy snorted. "I had no idea Charlotte had that kind of game."

Walker pondered that as he dug into the pot roast. Was that what had happened? Had Charlotte orchestrated their date? The more he found out about her, which wasn't that much so far, the more he was convinced that she was incredibly powerful.

If she was that powerful, had she already found the book? Seemed like a very real possibility. She could even be working on the Collective's end game right now.

And speaking of games, he was going to have to up his. He was not about to let a witch best him. Not when the fate of the world was at stake.

Chapter Four

"Edgar Allan...where are you? Mama's home." Charlotte put her keys in the bowl on the small table in her minuscule foyer, then toed off her ballet flats and walked into the kitchen in her stocking feet. The linoleum was cold, even through her tights. She shivered as she put her tote on the counter and took out her lunch bag.

Edgar Allan, her long-haired ginger cat, came trotting out of the bedroom and greeted her with a loud yowl.

She scooped him up and planted a kiss on his head. "Hello, my darling boy. How was your day?"

He started purring and bumped his head on her chin.

"That good? I'm so glad." She gave him a scratch, then set him down to get his dinner. Once she'd filled his bowl and he was happily eating, she put her lunch containers in the sink to wash later, then made herself a cup of cocoa. She thought about topping it with a handful of mini-marshmallows, but that was a little indulgent for a Wednesday. She took the rescued book out of her tote bag, then carried it and her plain cocoa into the living room.

She put both on the coffee table, tucked her feet under her, then picked up the book again. The cocoa was too hot to drink anyway. She ran her hand over the cover. The gold-embossed letters looked even less worn than they had in the library, and the leather seemed in remarkably good shape now. Not even a little tattered. Had she been mistaken about its condition at the library? Maybe she'd been so concerned with saving it, she hadn't been paying close attention to what it really looked like.

She brushed her thumb down the side of the bright gold pages. No glue that she could feel, but Millie hadn't been able to open it. Of course, Charlotte just took that as a challenge. She gripped the front cover and…the book opened easily.

"Well, how do you like that?" The pages were yellowed with time, and they rustled like dry leaves. She bit her lip. She ought to be wearing gloves like the kind they used to handle the historical documents in the library. Paper this delicate should be protected from the natural oils in her skin, but she didn't have any of those thin cotton gloves, just wool ones meant to keep her hands warm. She'd never be able to turn the pages wearing those.

She closed the book and put it back on the coffee table, then picked up her cocoa and drank some, giving herself time to think. Maybe her dish-washing gloves would work. They were rubber and the rubber was grippy. In theory, they might do the trick.

She set her mug down and went back to the kitchen. Edgar Allan was still at his food bowl, snarfing down the tuna pate she'd given him for dinner. Her gloves were under the sink, hanging over the PVC pipe that ran from her sink drain to wherever sink drains went to. She grabbed the gloves and went back to the book, tugging the gloves on as she sat. She wiggled her fingers in anticipation of looking through the pages without having to worry about the integrity of the tome.

A loud burp sounded from the kitchen.

She rolled her eyes even as she giggled. "Edgar Allan Poe Fenchurch, that is not very gentlemanly behavior."

He walked around the side of the couch and jumped up to settle onto the pillow at the far end. It was his spot really, and despite the fact that she kept a special pillowcase on that pillow that was washed on a regular basis, there was plenty of long ginger hair there to mark it.

She gave him the eye. "Are you done?"

He stuck his back leg over his head and began nonchalantly licking his inner thigh. He was done.

She went back to the book. She picked it up again, weighing it slightly in her hands. The feel of a book like this was really something. Hefty and solid, like it had pounds of interesting things inside. Which she had no doubt it did. Even if some of those things were potentially dark magic that she would not be bothering with.

Placing it on her lap, she grabbed the cover again and pulled.

The book wouldn't open.

That was odd. She turned it to better examine the pages. They seemed to have lost a bit of their shine. And upon closer inspection, the cover seemed old again. Even the title was now worn off in spots.

Weird.

On a hunch, she took the gloves off, then put her hands on the book again. The cover renewed its youthful exterior before her eyes. She gasped. "Magic. For protection maybe. I should have known with a book like this."

And if the cover had reverted to its previous appearance, then maybe... She took hold of the cover and opened the book without the slightest bit of resistance.

She closed it and opened it again. Then a third time just to be sure. She stared at the book's cover, a little amazed.

A sudden tingle of joy shot through her. She'd heard about things like this, about magical objects choosing the witch they wanted to belong to. She grinned and hugged the book to her chest. "And you chose me," she breathed out.

She was torn between calling her mentor and digging into the book immediately. Oh, she knew better than to attempt any of the questionable spells or even think she was ready for a book like this, but in time she would be. For parts of it anyway. And that was a thrilling thought.

Her first grimoire.

It was a momentous occasion. It called for a little celebration. She was having those mini-marshmallows after all.

She put the book on the table, then took her mug into the kitchen and popped it into the microwave for a quick warm-up while she got the marshmallows out.

The microwave dinged, followed by the sound of cathedral bells ringing on a loop. She stopped mid-reach for the microwave handle. Her phone was going off.

She dug into the side pocket of her tote bag. The number wasn't familiar, but she answered it anyway. "Hello?"

"Hello there, Charlotte."

That voice. She knew it by the lovely tremble it sent down her spine. It was Walker Black's voice. But she wasn't about to let him know she recognized him. Or the effect his voice had on her. "Who is this?"

"Oh, I'm wounded that you don't remember me. It's Walker Black."

She remembered him just fine. "Mr. Black. How did you get my number?"

"I looked you up. The Internet's an amazing thing. And please, call me Walker."

He'd Googled her? That was a little stalkery. But she would have done the same thing. She squinted into the distance. "How did you know my last name?"

"Library website. Charlotte Fenchurch, librarian. Likes include lobster rolls, walks along the coast, and rainy days spent indoors with a good book and a sleeping cat."

She frowned. "It does not say that about me." But he'd guessed very well. "How did you know I have a cat?"

"Took a swing based on the long orange hairs on the bottom of your skirt."

She glanced down at the hem of her navy plaid wool skirt. The right side had a small swathe of Edgar Allan fur clinging to it. She sighed. And gave Walker points for observation. "He does tend to shed." But then she remembered who she was talking to. "Why are you calling me at…" She checked the time. "Seven forty-two in the evening?" Or at all, really.

"Because I finished the book."

She looked at the time again. "You expect me to believe that you've done nothing but read all day? A romance novel?"

"No. I did stop to eat. Pot roast special at Chick-adee's. Have you had it? It's very good."

She had. It *was* good. And enough for three meals. Just the thought of it made her stomach rumble. She'd been too excited about the book to eat anything for dinner yet. "I have, but it sounds like you're changing the subject."

"I promise, I'm not. You said we could have coffee and discuss the book when I was done. Well, I'm done."

"And you want to talk about the book now?"

"Over coffee. And blueberry crumble. The last two pieces in the entire town of Everlasting are sitting at Chickadee's with my name on them. They're paid for and waiting on us."

"Oh, Chickadee's blueberry crumble. That is also very good." Now her mouth was watering along with her rumbling stomach. "I suppose that would be okay."

"Meet you in ten minutes?"

Ten minutes? She was still wearing her work

clothes. That would not do. Not when he'd noticed cat hair on her skirt. She needed to make him understand that she was not just a boring librarian. She wanted him to see her as a real person. Not a stereotype. Why that was suddenly so important, she wasn't sure, but that's how she felt. "Fifteen."

***

WALKER MADE it to the diner in eight. Betsy was still there, but the dinner crowd was mostly gone. Just a few stragglers hung on, some nursing coffee and pie that wasn't blueberry. He gave her a nod as he came in.

She smiled at him. "Back for the crumble?"

"Yes, but I'm going to grab a booth." He winked at her. "Meeting someone."

Her smile turned knowing. "I'll be right over."

He walked to the back and slid into the corner booth.

Charlotte showed up ten minutes later, making her three minutes late, but he forgot all about that as she walked toward him, looking very different than she had at the library. The simple skirt and blouse were gone, replaced by snug jeans tucked into riding boots and a tight, fuzzy sweater that made her seem like she had a soft glow about her. Her hair looked freshly brushed and the warm brown shone like rich, bourbon-laced caramel.

Witchcraft. He knew that. Knew what witches were capable of, especially one with Charlotte's gifts, but man, it knocked him back to see her go from prim librarian to…whatever this hotness was in front of him.

She looked very girl-next-door, rather than blatantly sexy, which didn't seem like her style anyway. But girl-next-door was a look he definitely had a weakness for.

Maybe she'd cast some kind of spell to figure that out about him. He wouldn't be surprised. And it was a good reminder of how tough an opponent he was up against. If she *was* an opponent, which he still hoped she wasn't.

She stopped at the edge of the booth. "Hello."

"Hello." He gestured to the empty banquette across from him. "Join me."

She slid in, putting her handbag on the seat beside her. "You really finished the book?"

"I really finished the book." He'd never read so fast in his life. But he'd had to see her again. Had to find out more about her and determine just how powerful she was. He needed a better measure of who this woman was and what kind of witch he was dealing with.

Betsy arrived and added a set of napkin-rolled silverware to each of their place mats. She dug her order book out of her apron and held her pen at the ready. "What can I get you kids? Besides the blue-berry crumble."

Walker looked to Charlotte.

She glanced up at Betsy. "Just a decaf, please."

"You got it." Betsy turned to Walker. "Decaf for you, too?"

"I'll take regular." Caffeine didn't affect him. And he might not be sleeping tonight anyway. He leaned back. "What's your advice on going ala mode with the crumble?"

Betsy smiled. "I can pop it in the microwave. Warm crumble with a scoop of vanilla bean? That'll cure what ails you."

"Let's do it."

Charlotte raised her hand. "Just the crumble for me."

"C'mon," Walker said. "No ice cream? That's no fun."

"No extra calories either." Charlotte shrugged. "This is technically my second dessert of the evening, so really, I'm good with just the crumble."

"All right." Betsy sighed like Charlotte had disappointed her and walked back behind the counter.

Charlotte folded her hands on the table. "All right, tell me. What did you think of *The Scoundrel Prince*?"

"It was…" Walker laughed softly, his eyebrows

twitching with how much the answer surprised him. "So much better than I expected."

She broke out into a big smile. "Really?"

"Absolutely. For one thing, I could see the whole thing in my head like a movie, you know? Regency London in all its grit and glory."

"And Lady Regina? And Lord Julian? What did you think of them?" Her eyes were sparkling with excitement.

It was very endearing. Books were clearly her passion. He loved that. But it didn't help her case. A witch who loved books was the perfect recipient for a grimoire like Middian's. He did his best to focus on the conversation at hand, sitting back to evaluate Lord Julian's character. "Well, he was an ass. At first anyway."

"Right, but he had all that baggage to overcome."

"For sure. Man, what a background. I mean, his mother – wow. And Regina was about as perfect as a woman could be. She definitely was the right one for him. I loved how she stood up to him. Told him exactly what he needed."

"I agree. She was perfect. What did you think of the stable scene?"

Walker frowned and thought back through what he'd read. He'd read fast, but he hadn't skimmed. "I hate to admit this, but I don't remember a stable scene."

Charlotte slapped her hand on the table top. "Because there wasn't one. That was a trick question."

His brows lifted. "You were testing me?"

She lifted one shoulder. "Don't get grumpy. You passed."

Chapter Five

Charlotte almost laughed at the disbelief on Walker's face. Had he really thought she wasn't going to try to trip him up? It was easy enough to fake that you'd read a book these days. All you had to do was go online and skim through the reviews. A lot of them were basically book reports, but they didn't cover the fine points. And she knew the book well enough to know it in full detail. Good on him for actually reading the book and for telling the truth. If he'd been lying, he would have just nodded and talked about how enjoyable the stable scene was, or something to that effect.

He hmphed as the waitress showed up with the coffee. "If I tell you I've done something, I've done it."

"So I see." She was still amused by his righteous indignation.

The waitress, Betsy, deposited two cups of steaming coffee onto the table. "Unleaded for you." She slid one toward Charlotte, then the second one in Walker's direction. "And leaded for you."

She pulled a handful of creamers out of her apron pocket and plopped them in the center of the table. "Be right back with the crumble."

Charlotte reached for two of the creamers. If Walker was a little put off by her quiz, she was okay with that. She didn't care what he thought about her. This wasn't a date. It was…something else. Coffee. And pie. But not a date. Because he wasn't her type, and she definitely wasn't his. "What else did you like about the book?"

Betsy returned before he could answer. She set a plate in front of each of them, and Charlotte had a small pang of regret, or possibly jealousy, when she saw the generous scoop of vanilla ice cream melting over his blueberry crumble. "There you go. Enjoy."

As Betsy left, Walker picked up his fork. His gaze held a subtle coolness that hadn't been there before. "Are you genuinely interested in what I liked about it, or is this another test?"

"Genuinely interested." She took her fork in hand. "Testing has concluded for this evening."

He snorted. "Well, in that case…the love scenes were very moving."

Her cheeks heated and she was powerless to stop it. The love scenes in *The Scoundrel Prince* were modestly detailed, but imaginative and filled with the sort of phrasing that left no doubt as to what was going on. They were some of the best that had ever been written in a romance novel, in Charlotte's opinion, and she'd read quite a few.

He pointed his fork at her, complete with a hunk of pie and a dollop of ice cream on the tines. "You're quiet. Does that mean you disagree?"

"No, I agree. They're, uh, masterful. An excellent example of how restrained language can paint a vivid picture." She quickly scooped up a mouthful of pie and ate it, eager for an excuse not to say more.

But the blueberry crumble was too good to be silent about. No wonder people raved whenever it came up.

She looked from the pie to Walker. He still hadn't eaten any. "Put that fork in your mouth already. This crumble is amazing."

He did. A second later, his eyes closed and a soft "Mmm" came out of him. It was a sound that caused a curious tingle in Charlotte. Not that it was so difficult to figure out. Especially coming on the heels of their love scene discussion. He swallowed, opening his eyes. "Wow. That's good."

"I'll say." She took another bite, savoring it this time and trying not to focus on the way pleasure made Walker's face even more handsome.

His brows pulled together in a questioning

expression. "Haven't you had this before? You do live here, after all."

She shook her head. "I don't eat out a lot. A librarian's salary isn't exactly lavish."

"Oh. I guess not." He tipped his head. "But you must go out on dates. Or is this not a date place?"

"No, it's a date place. I guess. I don't know. I don't go on many dates."

The furrow of his brows deepened. "Are you putting me on?"

"No, not at all." She poked at the pie with her fork. "I don't get asked. Okay, I get asked once in a while. But not very often."

"Why not?"

She sighed. "I don't think the male population thinks I'm that interesting."

"Then they're idiots. But you said you get asked once in a while, so when was the last time?"

"Doesn't count." She sipped her coffee. Also good.

"Why not?"

"Because my last date wasn't really a date. I was my cousin's plus one at another cousin's wedding."

"You're right. That probably doesn't qualify as a real date. At least it shouldn't." He ate more crumble. "You have a lot of family around here, then?"

"Not really. They're mostly in Boston."

"What brought you to Everlasting?"

"The library job."

"How long have you been here?"

"Almost four years." She forked up another piece of pie. "What brought you to Everlasting? Just the Festival?"

"Sort of. I'm an antiquer."

That stopped her short. "You're a what?"

"You know, I buy and sell antiques."

"I know what an antiquer is, but…" That was exactly what he didn't look like. Then she realized he was teasing her. "Come on. What are you really doing here?"

"I just told you. I go town by town through all the antique shops and search for hidden gems. I hit up estate sales, yard sales, thrift shops…you'd be amazed at what I find. A lot of it needs restoration, but that's part of what I do. Probably the part I like best."

"Then why have you been in the library so much?"

"You noticed that, huh?" He smiled. "When I find something interesting, that I don't know enough about, I research it. Also, I like to read. But the research helps me put a better price on things."

She immediately thought about the book. She had no interest in selling it, but it might be fun to know the value of it as an ordinary object. If it was really worth something, she'd add it to her renter's insurance. "Do you do appraisals?"

He nodded. "Sometimes. Mostly if someone's

looking to sell something. And between us, those people always want way more than what the thing is actually worth." He used the spoon from his coffee, which he took black, to scoop melted ice cream back onto his pie. "Why? You have something you want appraised?"

She lifted one shoulder. "I was kind of thinking about it. Depends on how much you charge."

He looked up from the crumble. "Dinner."

"Hmm?"

He smiled, but for the first time there was no confidence behind it. Charlotte found his sudden tentativeness engaging. "You could make me dinner the night I come over to do the appraisal." He glanced down at his plate. "The food here is good, but there's nothing like home cooked."

She snorted. "You're assuming I know how to cook."

The self-assurance she was used to seeing in his eyes returned. "Of course you're a good cook. For one thing, you love books and you told me that includes cookbooks."

"I also told you I'm no chef."

He waved the comment away. "Just you being modest. For another, you just told me your librarian's salary doesn't allow for a lot of eating out. That means you know how to feed yourself. Which means you can probably feed me too. And I'm happy to bring wine and a dessert."

He wasn't wrong. Which sort of irritated her that he was analyzing her, but it pleased her at the same time that he was paying attention. There was something special about a man who took notice of the things a woman said.

She sat back and crossed her arms. It would really be interesting to know what the book was worth. And also spend a little more time with Walker, who was actually a pretty decent guy. Even if he was out of her league. And not her type. "It won't be fancy."

His grin broadened. "Do I look like a fancy guy to you?"

"I'm serious. Spaghetti and garlic bread."

"Perfect. I'll bring red wine and tiramisu."

"Are you making that tiramisu?"

He laughed. "I'll be making the trip to Frisiello's to buy it. Does that count?"

Against her better judgment, she chuckled. "Half credit."

Frisiello's had amazing tiramisu, among other things. They were sort of the go-to spot in town for fancy Italian food. Something she only knew because she'd won dinner for two there in last year's Cranberry Festival raffle.

"Half credit is better than no credit. I'll take it." He angled his fork at her. "Tomorrow night, then?"

"I suppose. But…how do I know you're not a serial killer?"

He shot her a look. "How do I know *you're* not a serial killer?"

"You don't, but the odds are in your favor. Women only make up fifteen percent of the serial killer population."

"Is that so? In that case, I hope I don't get lucky."

She snorted before she could stop herself.

He leaned in. "Here's what you do. Tell everyone you know I'm coming over. Make it public knowledge. Have your friends call you throughout the night to check up on you. Maybe tell the cops to do a drive-by. Post it on social media. Invite a friend over. Whatever makes you comfortable is fine by me."

She smirked, but she was actually going to do a couple of those. "All right. Tomorrow night. Eight o'clock." Maybe she'd light a candle for protection, just like she was going to light a love candle for Millie when she got home. Couldn't hurt. Unless she used the *ustulo* spell again and incinerated the building. If she didn't perfect that spell soon, she was going to get arrested for accidental arson.

He forked up the last bit of his pie. "Then it's a date. Our second, to be exact."

And just like that, she realized that despite everything she'd wanted to think, a date was exactly what she'd been on in the first place.

Chapter Six

The next night, Walker showed up at the address Charlotte had texted him. He had a couple minutes to spare, but that was just being smart. It gave him a chance to scope the place out.

Not much to scope. She lived in a small apartment building built in the very economical New England salt box style. Its twin sat beside it, divided by a strip of common area that had a path worn through from foot traffic. Each chalk-white building had three floors, faded blue trim around the windows and narrow balconies served by a set of sliding doors.

Two single-bulb street lamps lit the small parking lot, but the buildings had security lights at the corners and at the stair landings on each floor. The right-hand building wore a sign that said

Seaview One. The left hand, Seaview Two. Neither had an actual sea view.

The only other interesting note was the slight sourness of dark magic. It was a common smell and pretty much everywhere these days. So common he often ignored it unless he was on a mission. Which he was. And in an apartment complex, there was no telling what might be going on in some of those rooms. But then again, it could be an indicator that the book was here.

He'd know for sure very soon.

Charlotte lived in Seaview One, apartment 2D. He took the wine and boxed tiramisu out of his truck, then headed up to the second floor.

The aroma of spaghetti sauce met him as he approached, wiping out the sourness he'd picked up in the parking lot. Garlic and the sweetness of tomatoes, plus something herby. Oregano or basil maybe. She was cooking for him, and he was here to determine once and for all if she was the enemy or just a hapless pawn of the Collective. Didn't seem quite fair. He really hoped she was the later. And if she was the first, he also hoped she wasn't putting any potions or poisons into his food. Wouldn't be the first time a witch had tried to take him out that way.

He raised his hand and knocked. He was glad he'd spent a bit extra on the wine. Even if Charlotte was potentially the enemy, something that was getting harder and harder to remember, he didn't think she got to experience the nicer things in life that often. At least not based on what she'd told him about her income and now seeing the place where she lived. That made him a little unhappy.

Of course, if this was all part of a ploy to hide who she really was, then he was a sap.

Charlotte answered. She was wearing an apron and wiping her hands on a kitchen towel. Her hair was twisted up in a clip, but a few pieces had fallen down to frame her pretty face. His stomach growled, but the delicious aromas were only partly to blame.

She smiled at him. "You're right on time. But I'm a smidge behind." She backed up so he could go in. "Sorry. It's been a long day."

"Everything okay?" The place was tiny, but warm and inviting. Their arms touched as he walked into the narrow foyer.

"Not really. Someone broke into the library last night and ransacked the place. There were books everywhere. They were pulled off the shelves and tossed around like someone was bent on destruction. It was a mess." She shut the door. "The sheriff came and there were deputies all over and it was nuts."

He already knew about the break-in. He'd been watching the library most of the day and taking photos of the patrons in case Charlotte wasn't on the Collective's payroll. Which, judging by her postage stamp apartment, was looking more and more likely. At least she wasn't on the big money side of the payroll. Unless she wasn't getting her reward until she handed over the book.

Then that payday might be enough incentive to sway her. Especially with how little she made at the library. And the Collective might worry that they'd need that incentive to keep her from holding on to the book for herself. But if she was the Collective's agent, why would she ransack the library? She had access to it anytime. The only reason he could think of was to send him hunting in the wrong direction. From that angle, trashing the library made perfect sense. He dug deeper. "Did they take anything? What did the sheriff find?"

"Not much. There was nothing missing that we could determine. The place was dusted for prints, which I then had to clean up." She sighed as she tossed the towel over her shoulder and went back into her tiny kitchen. "They took our fingerprints too, to compare them."

"Our? As in yours and the other woman who works there?" He put the wine and the dessert on the counter.

"Yes. And that other woman is the head librarian, Mildred Merriweather. We also have a part-timer, Norm Poole. Not sure what good the prints are going to do them, though. There's not a book in there the three of us haven't touched. And it's a public library. Everyone in town is going to have prints in there."

"True." Which meant the sheriff's department wasn't going to find anything helpful, but it was still a great way to cast aspersions elsewhere. He gently tapped the top of the tiramisu box. "Okay if I put this in the fridge?"

"Oh, sure." She blew her bangs off her forehead. "Sorry, I'm talking your ear off with my woes. How was your day?"

"I don't mind listening at all. My day was fine. Boring by comparison." People watching, while necessary, was not his idea of a good time. After taking pictures of everyone who'd visited the library today, he'd uploaded them to the FOL's cloud to be scanned against the database of Collective agents. Chances were slim a match would be returned, but any opportunity to shift things in his favor was one he would take.

Of course, he hadn't taken Charlotte's picture yet.

He opened the fridge and put the tiramisu on a shelf. Everything inside was precisely placed and neatly lined up. All the labels were faced out. Charlotte liked organization, apparently. He was good with that. Organization made life easier. He closed the fridge door. "Dinner smells great, by the way."

"Thanks." She shot him a quick smile as she slipped oven mitts on. "It's almost ready, too."

"Anything I can do to help?"

"Open that wine and pour us some glasses."

"I can definitely do that. Wine opener?"

"Drawer next to the fridge."

"On it. But first…" He pulled out his phone, tapped the camera, and held it up. "Let's get a selfie. I'll post it and you can like it or share it or whatever, then people will know we're hanging out."

"Sure. In case you turn out to be a serial killer."

"Exactly. This will give the police something to go on."

She laughed. "Okay, but it's a little unfair. You look great. Meanwhile, the steam from the pasta water has flattened my hair and melted my makeup."

"You look beautiful." It was out of his mouth before he could stop himself. It wasn't a lie. She did. But he shouldn't be saying things like that to a woman he might have to take into custody. "I just mean flattened hair and melted makeup is a good look for you."

She gave him a curious glance. "That's kind of you. But you don't have to flatter me. I'm already making you dinner. And I know the truth."

He took a harder look at her. She was beautiful. Maybe not in a Hollywood way, but interesting faces had always appealed to him far more than perfect ones. Although hers was pretty close to perfect. He leaned in, snapped the shot, then asked,

"What's that supposed to mean, you know the truth?"

She picked up the pasta pot and poured the contents into the strainer waiting in the sink. "I know what I look like. I'm no beauty queen. On a good day, I'm average. And that's okay. I'm kind and smart and occasionally funny. I'm one of those people whose good stuff is on the inside."

"You're selling yourself short." He sent the picture off to the cloud, then put his phone away.

She put the empty pot back on the stove, turned the heat off, and added the smaller, steaming pot of sauce to it. "And I think you're being kind again. Which is sweet, but unnecessary."

"Just being honest. And it's absolutely necessary."

She gave the strainer a shake, then dumped the pasta back into the pot with the sauce. Then she grabbed what he guessed was a loaf of foil-wrapped garlic bread she'd prepped earlier and popped it in the warm oven. "Well, that's nice of you, and forgive my skepticism, but I have a hard time buying a guy like you being interested in a woman like me."

"I don't really know what that means."

She rolled her eyes. "Walker, I hope you're not fishing for compliments. You have to know how good-looking you are. And from experience, I know guys who look like you don't go for women who look like me. It's just not how nature works."

That made him angry. Not at her, but that life had given her enough examples to make her think that was true. There was only one thing he could think of that would give her a reason to believe otherwise.

As the beast in him came to life, he did what he'd wanted to do since he'd first seen her. He leaned in and kissed her.

⁂

CHARLOTTE GASPED against Walker's mouth. She hadn't expected him to kiss her. Not in a million years.

Her second thought was there could be only one logical explanation as to why this was happening. The love candle she'd lit for Millie had gone terribly wrong. Somehow Charlotte must have made herself the focus of the spell. Or worse, she'd made Walker the focus of it. Which, yeah, was *bad*.

Her third thought was that maybe *terribly* wrong was not completely accurate. As mistakes went, this wasn't so awful. But if he was kissing her because of a spell she'd improperly cast, that was unfair to him. She was not the kind of woman to take advantage of a man inappropriately bewitched.

She pulled away. "That shouldn't have happened."

He frowned. "This *is* a date, you know."

"That's not what I meant. It's just that…you know what? Never mind." She couldn't exactly tell him she was a witch and that the reason he'd kissed her was the lingering after effects of a spell gone wrong. "It's fine. Forget I said anything."

"Oh. Good. Fine. That's what every man hopes to hear after kissing a woman." He rolled his eyes.

She laughed. "That's not what I meant. Not exactly. Although, the kiss was good. I think." She grimaced. All her thoughts about messing up the love candle had distracted her. "I wasn't totally paying attention."

He looked like she'd slapped him in the face with a filet of cod. "You weren't paying attention?"

"I was too overwhelmed with the shock of it all." That was a good cover. "I'm really sorry. I'm also a little preoccupied with the library being broken into and all that."

He shook his head. "I guess I can understand that. And it explains why you kissed me back with all the enthusiasm of a slab of Spam."

"What?" Now it was her turn to look like she'd been slapped. "I do not kiss like a slab of Spam."

His brows lifted and he shrugged. "Just telling you what it was like on my side. Pretty Spammy."

"That's…preposterous." She did not kiss like canned meat. Whatever that meant anyway. Her frustration grew with the smirk that appeared on his face.

He pursed his lips. "Hey, it's okay. Some people just aren't good kissers."

Her jaw dropped open. She might not have kissed a lot of men, but she'd never had any complaints before. She leaned in and planted one on him, giving it her full attention and best effort.

This time, Walker sucked in a surprised breath. She liked that she'd caught him off guard and after another few seconds of her mouth on his, she broke away, trying to look as cool as she could despite the heat curling through parts south. Were his eyes glowing? He blinked and it was gone, so it had to be a trick of the light.

She backed up, but kept a firm grip on the counter as a precaution against the weakness in her knees. "There. How was that?"

A second or two passed with him just staring at her, his mouth slack with what she assumed was the shock of her kissing him. Then he sort of shook himself and came around. "It was good. Better. Good. Not Spammy at all."

"See?" She turned back to the pot of pasta. "We should probably eat before this gets cold."

"Right."

She looked over her shoulder. He hadn't really moved. "You going to pour us that wine?"

"Huh? Oh, yes. Wine. On it." He found the opener in the drawer she'd directed him to earlier and got to work. He looked happy to have a task.

She knew the feeling. She got the garlic bread out of the oven and into a basket, then served up two dishes of spaghetti and carried all three to her very small table.

He joined her a second later with the glasses of wine. He handed her one. "Dinner looks great."

"Thank you."

He raised his glass. "Here's to new friends. And great books."

She smiled. "I like that. To new friends and great books." And if things went well, maybe one more kiss.

Chapter Seven

Most of dinner was spent talking about books, a subject that Walker had no trouble keeping Charlotte focused on. They talked about movies, too, and some of the people and places in town, but he steered the conversation back to books anytime she seemed about to ask him something personal.

He just didn't want to lie to her any more than he already had, and there was no way he could answer personal questions honestly.

Not after that first kiss. Which shouldn't have happened. Or that second one. Which *really* shouldn't have happened. Or maybe it was more that his reaction to it shouldn't have happened. The first kiss had only been to prove to her that he truly thought she was beautiful. But the second kiss? The second kiss had been completely unexpected. And it had done something dangerous to him.

Charlotte's sweet, innocent-but-determined effort had turned him inside out. It had awoken the beast inside him and it had taken everything he had not to react in an animalistic way. As it was, he was sure his eyes had glowed a little that second time.

He was used to the witches he hunted trying to use their feminine charms on him. This wasn't that. Nothing about Charlotte's kiss had been manipulative. It had been all about trying to prove him wrong, trying to show him that she was a good kisser.

And Hades take him, she was. Not good, but great. Soft but with the right amount of pressure, sweet but also a little daring, and tentative in that way that told him her inexperience did not mean she wasn't willing or interested in learning.

He was, to use a word, bewitched. And for the first time since meeting her, he didn't think magic had anything to do with it.

"You still with me?"

He looked up from his plate. "Sorry. Lost in thought for a second."

She nodded. "Happens to me all the time. What were you thinking about?"

A lie was the first thing that popped into his head, but he was still stuck on that kiss and honesty won out. "Us. In the kitchen."

She bit her lip and turned the sexiest shade of pink. "I don't usually behave like that."

"Oh?" He grinned. "Good to know you don't always take advantage of the men you invite over."

She let out an indignant little laugh-snort. "I did not take advantage of you. Not intentionally anyway. And technically, you invited yourself."

"Oh, well, not intentionally makes it all right." How could she have intentionally taken advantage of him? Witchcraft? Was that what she meant? He couldn't be sure, but it was a curious statement all the same. He used his garlic bread to wipe the last bit of sauce off his plate. "Dinner was outstanding."

"You know it was just a box of pasta and a jar of sauce, right?"

"Must have been the company that really put it over the edge."

She smiled. "Thanks. I think the company absolutely helped. The wine was very good, too."

"And dessert is yet to come. Although I need a few minutes before I eat anything else." He finally broached the subject of why he was there. "I'd be happy to look at that book for you, now. See if I can give you an idea of what it's worth."

"Sounds good to me." She stood and picked up their plates. "Let me clean up a little, start a pot of coffee, and then I'll go get it."

He got up from his chair. "I'll help with the dishes. Only fair."

"You're a guest."

"And, as you reminded me, the reason you went

to the effort of cooking." He gave her a wink, then went into the kitchen and started filling the sink with hot water. "Get the coffee going, then you can dry while I wash."

She put the dishes by the sink. "You're sure you don't mind?"

"Not a bit."

"You want gloves?"

He held his hands up in mock outrage. "These are the callused hands of a working man. I don't need gloves."

She raised her brows. "You get calluses antiquing?"

"Okay, calluses might be exaggerating, but antiquing isn't all I do." He grabbed the sponge and the dish soap off the back of the sink and went to work on the plates.

She emptied the remaining pasta and sauce into a large container and stuck it in the fridge. "What else do you do?"

These were the personal questions he'd been trying to avoid, but he'd started this conversation. She had him off his game, that was for sure. Thankfully, a few vague answers should do the trick. "I work on motorcycles. I'm rebuilding one now. It's an old Indian. A real classic."

She put the empty pasta pot next to the sink so he could wash it, then turned to the coffee maker behind them. "Did you find that in an antique store?"

"Estate sale, actually. In an outbuilding." He put the dishes on a towel for her to dry. "It hadn't been touched in ages. It was a mess but the bones were good. It was exactly the kind of project I was looking for."

"What will you do with it when it's done?" She stuck the carafe under the running faucet, watching the water until it hit the fill line.

"Drive it a little, but then sell it and find a new project."

"You like projects, huh?"

"I do. I get bored easily. A new project every couple of months keeps things interesting."

She got the coffee going, then walked around him to start drying the plates. "What's your favorite kind of antique to look for?"

"Anything that helps me pay the bills."

She laughed. "I can understand that. Do you ever think about having your own shop?"

"Not really. I like traveling too much." He tackled the pasta pot next. It wasn't that he loved traveling that much, but the FOL constantly sent him on missions. Traveling was part of his job, like it or lump it. "A shop would tie me down."

A little of the joy in her eyes disappeared. "Traveling sounds fun, but I don't think I could live my life like that. Too much of a homebody, I guess."

He studied her as he rinsed the pot. "As much as you like to read, have you ever thought about writing a book yourself?"

She narrowed her eyes. "Are you psychic?"

He laughed. "Why? Are you writing one?"

She nodded, her expression a little shy. "Yes. But I'm just dabbling. I don't think it's any good."

"I bet it's great." He handed the pot off to her. "What's it about?"

She shook her head. "I don't want to talk about it. It's not ready to talk about yet."

"Okay, I understand that." He finished up the last few things, then joined her in the drying. "You have to do what the work needs. But I'd think most importantly with a book, you have to let the story guide you in how it wants to be told."

"Motorcycle man, antiquer, washer of dishes, and now philosopher. You're quite the renaissance man, Walker."

"Hey, I have diverse interests."

"Apparently. But how do you know how a story needs to be told?"

He shrugged. "All the antiques I deal with have a story. I don't always get to know what that story is, but I try to be mindful of that when I'm cleaning a piece up. I don't want to take the story out of it, you know? In fact, what I'm really trying to do is let that story shine through even more."

She smiled. "I like that. I like that a lot." She

finished drying the silverware and put it away. The dark, delicious smell of brewing coffee filled the small space. "I'll go grab the book and meet you in the living room."

He hung up the towel he'd been using. "See you in there."

BECAUSE CHARLOTTE always erred on the side of caution, she'd brought home two pairs of the thin cotton gloves they used in the library. It wasn't stealing, because she was only borrowing them, but it was a precaution she had to take. She didn't want Walker to know she could open the book, or risk him seeing the spells inside. The only way to be sure of that was to keep from making direct contact.

And wearing dishwashing gloves wasn't going to be as easily explained as the cotton ones.

Of course, if he happened to be some kind of sorcerer himself and was able to open the book with his bare hands, the gloves would prevent that as well. Which probably wasn't even something she needed to be concerned about, but she liked to plan for everything. Living in Everlasting had taught her that much.

She put one pair of gloves on, then went to get the book. It was on the top shelf of her closet. Edgar Allan was curled up on the bed, completely zoned out. No wonder he hadn't come out during dinner. She chuckled at him, then got the book down, laid the second pair of gloves on the cover, and carried the whole lot out to Walker.

"Here it is." She put the book on the coffee table. "If you don't mind, I'd like you to wear the gloves while you examine it. Maybe it's valuable, maybe it's not, but it's still a very old book and I'd like to preserve it as best as I can."

"Sure." He picked up the gloves and slipped them on. "I tend to wear gloves when doing a lot of my restoration work. It's a good precaution when dealing with delicate things."

She sat beside him on the couch. Not too close, but close enough to be a part of what he was doing. "Like I said, even if it's not worth anything, I still want to preserve it. I'm pretty sure it's the oldest book I've ever owned. I feel like that deserves some respect." It was also her first grimoire, which made it exceedingly special, but she couldn't explain that to him.

He glanced over at her. "You really like books, don't you? More than just for reading."

She nodded. "I do." She shifted her gaze to the book on the table. "Books have kept me company all my life. They've allowed me to explore inter-esting places when my budget wouldn't. Experience new things. Meet strange, wonderful people. I can't imagine my life without them."

He smiled. "Good thing, considering your job."

She laughed. "Right. Which is another thing I have books to thank for."

"Okay, let's have a look at this one." He picked up the book and turned it over, studying the cover from all angles.

She waited patiently while he inspected the outside. She knew he probably wasn't seeing the cover the same way she was, but Charlotte wanted to test that theory. "Pretty rough, right? You can hardly read the title."

"Right." He shot her a quick, indecipherable look. "But that could be restored." He put his hands on the sides and pulled. Nothing.

She almost sighed in relief.

He frowned. "Pages are stuck together. That's unfortunate." He shook his head. "Pretty much makes the book worthless."

Which was what she'd expected him to say. "Oh well, it's still pretty. To me anyway. I'm happy to have it on my shelf no matter what it looks like."

He put the book back on the coffee table and took the gloves off. "If you're going to keep it, I could restore that cover for you. Redo the gold leafing on the title, touch up the leather in a few spots, that sort of thing. Wouldn't take me more than a day."

"That's kind of you, and I really appreciate the

offer, but I'm okay with how it looks." Especially because it didn't look like that to her.

"You're sure? I don't mind doing it."

A glimmer of something lit his gaze. Frustration? Disappointment? She couldn't tell. She picked the book up, hugging it to her chest with her gloved hands. "I'm sure. I'm also sure I'm ready for dessert. I'll just go put this back, then we'll dig into that tiramisu you brought."

He got up at the same time she did. "Okay, I'll get it out of the fridge."

She took off for her bedroom while he headed to the kitchen, meeting him back there a few minutes later.

He had the box of tiramisu out and had found cups for the coffee and small plates for the dessert, plus two forks. "I looked through the cabinets for these. I hope that's okay."

She shrugged. "Sure. Not like I'm hiding state secrets in there or anything." She peeked into the box. He'd gotten two pieces, which was perfect. "Wow, does that look good."

"I hope so." He used the forks to lift each piece onto a plate, then picked up the plates. "I'll take these to the table."

"Right behind you." She got the creamer carton from the fridge and took it and the sugar bowl out, then came back, filled both cups with coffee and brought them to the table as well. She sat and started fixing her coffee. "What are you doing tomorrow?"

"Checking out Cavanaugh's Antique Mall."

She laughed as she stirred her coffee. "I think you're going to be disappointed. It should be called Cavanaugh's Crap Mall."

"That bad, huh?"

She nodded and picked up her fork. "Maybe you'll find something. Who knows? But don't haggle too much. Crazy Cavanaugh is one of those cranky New Englanders who'd just as soon run you out of his place than give you a nickel off."

"Good to know. Anything else I should know about him?"

"Just that you'd be better off at Hunted Treasures Antiques. If you go by there, the owner's name is Wilber Messing. He's a really nice guy and one of the regulars at the library. Tell him I sent you." Maybe if Walker bought something, Wilber would give her a little extra off that crystal ball she'd been eyeing.

"Will do."

They ate, the tiramisu indeed as good as it looked, and she told him some more colorful stories about the people and places in town.

With the tiramisu gone, Charlotte was about to clean up, but just then Edgar Allan came sauntering out of the bedroom.

Walker's head came up. "I knew you said you had a cat, but I was picturing something…"

"Smaller?" She laughed. "He's kind of a beast, but he's my beast. Aren't you, baby? At least he finally stopped sleeping and came out to say hi. Edgar Allan, say hello to Mr. Walker Black."

"He's quite the handsome fellow. Is Edgar Allan after Poe?"

"Yes." She liked that Walker knew the reference. Not that Edgar Allan Poe was so hard to guess, but not everyone got it.

Edgar Allan paused a few feet from Walker. He arched his back, and a low yowl spilled out of him like a feline warning.

"Edgar Allan, stop that," Charlotte said. "Walker is a guest."

"It's okay. I'm invading his territory." Walker held his hand out for Edgar Allan to sniff. "Sorry about that, big man. But I'm not an enemy, I promise."

The cat stretched his neck out and sniffed Walker's hand. He hissed once, softly, then sniffed again. This time, he rubbed his cheek on Walker's fingers.

Walker grinned. "See? Friends."

She watched with interest. "Huh. He's never reacted like that with anyone before."

Apparently satisfied that the intruder was no foe, Edgar Allan trotted off to the couch to take up his favorite spot.

Walker stood. "I'm glad he likes me. I'd hate to leave on a sour note."

"You're leaving?" The evening had gone by so fast.

"It's getting late, and we both have work tomorrow. Speaking of, how about we hit Chickadee's for dinner when you get done at the library?"

That would be their second date. Or third, since Walker seemed to think the coffee counted. She almost hesitated, but it wasn't like she had anything else to do. "Okay. I can meet you there around seven twenty. How's that?"

"Perfect. I'll be waiting."

They both got to their feet and she walked him to the door. "Thanks for the wine and dessert. It was great."

"So was dinner. Thanks, again." He opened the door, then leaned in and gave her another kiss on the mouth. "See you tomorrow, Charlotte."

A little wobbly-kneed from the over-too-soon kiss, she nodded. "Tomorrow."

Then he was out the door and gone, and she was alone to think about what on earth she was doing with a man like Walker.

Chapter Eight

Charlotte had the book.

That was Walker's last thought as he fell asleep and his first thought when he woke up. He stared at the pitched ceiling. The room was still dark, as the sun had yet to crack the horizon, but his shifter eyes didn't need much light to see by. He had work to do. He knew that. But he remained in bed, thinking about last night's date.

He'd hoped his dinner with Charlotte would help him determine which side she was on. It hadn't really. All it had confirmed was her possession of Middian's.

And that he liked her far more than he should.

He sighed. Nothing about her demeanor or personality made him think she was remotely the type of person who might be recruited by the

Collective. Sure, she needed money, but she didn't strike him as desperate for it. And yes, she was a witch, but other than the second kiss they'd shared, there wasn't one spot in the evening where he'd felt as though she'd deliberately been using magic on him.

That *kiss*, though. It had stuck in his head. So much so that she'd shown up in his dreams to kiss him again. He ran his fingers over his mouth. The soft, insistent press of her lips and the tantalizing warmth of her breath lingered as though she was right there with him.

No, that kiss had been too pure to have been magic.

Or it might have been magic more powerful than anything he'd come up against. And Charlotte might be the craftiest witch he'd run into. Did she know what he was? After all, she hadn't let him take the book, even after he'd generously offered to restore it.

He bounced his fist on the bed.

Charlotte was a puzzle. A beautiful, sexy puzzle he wanted to get to know piece by piece.

His phone vibrated. He picked it up off the nightstand and checked the screen. Stillwell. Walker answered. "Morning, boss."

"The mission's changed. Bring in the book and the witch."

No hello, no how are you, no small talk. That

was Stillwell. "What do you mean *and the witch*?"

"Bring her in with the book."

Walker sat up. "The last time the FOL asked me to bring in a witch was when I was hunting that woman who was hexing telemarketers with the throat-closing sickness. Charlotte isn't doing anything like that. I don't even know yet if she's actually working for the Collective or not."

"The order's been given. Bring her – and the book – in." Stillwell hung up.

A rare swell of rebellion turned Walker's vision temporarily red. He'd known taking Charlotte in had been a possibility, but now it was an order. That grinded his gears. Taking her in would disrupt her life in a way that meant it would never be the same. Guilty witches who were taken into custody rarely saw the light of day again.

He'd been to the FOL's holding cells once, when he'd delivered Elmira Boudreaux, the bane of telemarketers everywhere. She'd killed three of those telemarketers just for doing their jobs, and all because they'd dared to interrupt her dinner. Elmira deserved to be locked away from the world for her crimes and the use of dark magic, but Charlotte hadn't done anything. At least that he knew about.

Just the thought of her in those dark, isolated, magic-proofed cells made him shudder.

He was torn. He'd never disobeyed an order.

But he'd never been given an order he felt was so blatantly wrong.

Then again, he'd never kissed a witch he'd been sent to hunt. Not that he'd really been sent to hunt Charlotte, but she was certainly a part of this whole mess. In some way.

He shook his head. He had to get some answers today. And that meant talking to Charlotte. But the library wouldn't be open for another three hours. He decided to go out for a run. Sometimes that helped him think.

By the time he got back, the sun was up, but his decision to talk to Charlotte hadn't changed. He would be at the library when it opened. He had to return *The Scoundrel Prince* anyway. But he still had two hours to kill. He took his laptop out and checked the FOL database to see if any of the pictures he'd taken yesterday had matched with any potential Collective agents.

Not a one. Including Charlotte's. That just fueled his annoyance. There was no reason for the FOL to want her, too.

He put his laptop away, showered and dressed, then headed to Chickadee's. Might as well see how the breakfast was.

Turned out to be as good as he'd expected, and a stack of cranberry pancakes, two eggs, home fries, and three strips of bacon later, Walker was ready to talk to Charlotte and find out which side she was on.

It would be good to see her. It felt like it had been ages.

He got to the library thirty minutes before opening, so he positioned himself on the bench outside the front door and waited, but not for long.

Charlotte was early, which didn't surprise him. The look on her face when she saw him was a little more unexpected. He thought after last night she'd be happy to see him. Instead, her brows knit in an expression of displeasure. "Hi. What are you doing here?"

Yeah, not the welcome he'd expected. Maybe she wasn't a morning person. Good thing he'd brought her breakfast. He picked up the coffee and the waxed paper bag holding the takeout order he'd gotten. "I need to talk to you, but I also brought you breakfast. There's a cranberry orange muffin and an egg sandwich in there. I wasn't sure which one you'd prefer, so I got both."

She smiled. A little.

He lifted the cup higher. "Skinny caramel latte. I took a chance."

"That sounds really good. I never get takeout coffee. Too expensive. Anyway, that was nice of you." She chewed on her bottom lip. "Millie won't like it, though."

"That I brought you coffee?"

"No, that I'm having a personal visitor while I'm at work."

So that was it. He grinned as he got to his feet. "But this isn't just a personal visit. I also need to return *The Scoundrel Prince*, so that makes it partially an official visit."

Her smile widened. "That's good. And maybe you could look for another book to check out? Make it even more official?"

"I can do that." Then he could get her away from the front desk and into the stacks to discuss her role in all this. That was about as private as it was going to get while she was at work, but he'd have to risk it.

"Excellent." She had a key in her hand. "Let me get the lights on and get through the opening routine, then you can come in. Shouldn't be more than twenty minutes or so." She looked over her shoulder. "Judge Turnbury will probably show up soon. He's usually waiting on me when I open the doors. Although he's never brought me breakfast."

Walker smiled at her last comment. "When does Millie get here?"

Charlotte turned the key in the lock. "Any minute, but she has a reserved spot in the back. Which is the way she comes in too." Charlotte bumped the door open with her hip, hoisting the straps of her tote bag higher on her shoulder, then she reached over and took the coffee cup and takeout bag from him and winked. "Thanks. See you in a few."

He nodded, a little dazzled by the wink. That wasn't good. A wink wasn't anything to be dazzled by, not under normal circumstances. He was definitely under her spell.

He sighed and sat back down on the bench. There was no way a witch as powerful as Charlotte was going to let herself be taken into custody. Not without a helluva fight.

"THERE ARE PATRONS WAITING," Millie announced as she strode into the library from the back.

Charlotte jumped at the sound of her voice, almost spilling the very delicious coffee Walker had brought her. Fortunately, she'd already scarfed down the muffin. She turned from the break room fridge where she was putting her lunch away. "I'm getting ready to open right now, but I didn't realize we had a crowd."

"Not a crowd, just one actually. But more could be coming any time. Judge Turnbury will show up any second."

Charlotte almost rolled her eyes. Millie loved to exaggerate when it suited her purposes. "The judge's arthritis must be bothering him again. It's not like him to be late. And I know the man who's out there waiting now, and he's fine waiting until we're ready to open."

"Even so, our sign states we open at nine."

"We will. It's 8:53."

Millie put her handbag into the cubby that was reserved for her. "I have a conference call with the Maine Library Association about the upcoming general meeting and this charity grant we may potentially be getting, so I'll be in my office most of the morning."

Charlotte nodded. "Great. Sounds like fun." It really didn't, but she would gladly take the call if it meant she was head librarian and Millie wasn't in the equation anymore. Not that she wished Millie any ill fortune, but the woman could be a bit much at times. Of course, becoming head librarian after Millie wasn't a guarantee. The Maine Library Association could always promote another more experienced librarian from another branch. "The front desk will be handled."

Millie raised her chin slightly. "I expect nothing less. Today's papers need to be put out, too."

As if Charlotte didn't do that every morning. She barely restrained a second eye roll. "Yep, I'll make sure that's done as well."

Millie went to fix her morning cup of tea. "All right then, get those doors open."

"Going." Some days, Charlotte couldn't wait until she was the head librarian of her own library.

Although at times, Charlotte wondered if she'd make it that long with Millie for a boss. With a soft sigh, she grabbed her coffee and headed to the front. Walker was patiently waiting. Judge Turnbury was shuffling up the walk, so that answered the question of whether he was okay. She opened the door and gave Walker a quick look, which he returned just as discreetly. Then she greeted the judge and stood there, holding the door while she waited for him to get through it. "Morning, Judge."

"Morning, Charlotte."

He smelled of liniment. Poor man. His arthritis must really be acting up. Getting old was no fun. "I'll have the day's paper for you in a just a minute."

He nodded as he trundled into the library. "Take your time, take your time."

Walker came in after him, but paused as he reached Charlotte. "Do what you need to do. I'll be looking for my next book."

"Okay. Thanks. I'll find you when I'm free." Which would take all of three minutes. Sure, there were still things that needed doing. But Millie was holed up in her office, and Walker needed to talk to her. And he'd brought her fancy coffee. And food.

After a quick buzz by Millie's office to make sure she was actually in there, and the trip to the reading room to bring the judge his paper, Charlotte found Walker in the science fiction row. She sidled up to him, keeping her voice to a whisper even though

Judge Turnbury was on the other side of the building and the only other patron in the place. Not to mention a little hard of hearing. "So, what's up?"

Walker shelved the Isaac Asimov omnibus he was perusing and faced her. The stern set of his mouth and the strength of his gaze made her think something serious was about to happen. "This isn't where I wanted to do this, but time is running out."

"Time for what?" His tone was grave, but she didn't have a clue what he was talking about.

He took hold of her hand, his fingers loosely wrapping her wrist. "Listen, I know you're a witch. But what I don't know is who you're working for. I need you to tell me."

She jerked her head back. "Now I really don't know what you're talking about. And how do you know I'm a witch?"

"Are you working for the Collective? Have they contacted you?" He was peering at her intensely.

"Who's the Collective? And why would they contact me? The only organization I work for is the Maine Library system."

"You're telling the truth." He let go of her wrist.

"Of course I'm telling the truth." She was also starting to get a little mad. "What is going on?"

He glanced past her, like he was checking for eavesdroppers. "That book you had me look at? It's not worthless. It's very valuable and very powerful."

"I know."

He frowned. "How?"

"Well, like you said, I'm a witch—"

"But if you can't open it, it won't do you any good."

She crossed her arms. "Who said I can't open it?"

Chapter Nine

Charlotte's words hit Walker like a gut punch. "You can open the book?"

"Yes. But only when I have direct contact with it."

He couldn't believe what he was hearing, but it all made sense. "That's why you wore the gloves. And made me wear them." Wow. Charlotte *was* crafty.

"Yes." Then she shrugged. "Why is it such a big deal that I can open the book?"

"Because...it is." He didn't want to explain to her everything that meant. Not standing in the middle of a public library. "I need you to give me—"

"Hello? Anyone here?"

Charlotte whipped around toward the voice. "Coming!" She marched off toward the front desk.

"Wait—" But she was already moving. Walker stayed on her heels. She was surprisingly quick. "Charlotte, I—"

"Sheriff Bull." Charlotte slipped behind the front desk and put on a big smile. "Done with that Reacher book already?"

"No, no, this is business." The sheriff frowned. "I'm sorry to say but there's been another break-in."

Charlotte looked confused. "Not here."

The sheriff sighed and put her hands on her belt. "No. Unfortunately, it was at your apartment."

"What?" Charlotte sucked in a sharp breath. Her knuckles went white where she was holding onto the edge of the counter. "*Edgar Allan.* Is my cat okay?"

"Yes, he's just fine. But we need you to come with us and identify what's been taken."

She nodded like she was numb. "Okay. H-how did you find out about the break-in?"

"Your neighbor saw that the lock had been jimmied."

"They must have been waiting for me to leave for the library." Charlotte looked at her watch. "I've only been gone forty-five minutes."

They'd made quick work of the place, Walker thought.

"Sounds like that's exactly what happened," the sheriff said.

"You think it was the Belmont brothers?" Charlotte asked. "You know those two are shady."

"Could be. We'll know when we run the prints." The sheriff tipped her head slightly. "Why don't you ride with me?"

"I'll drive her," Walker said.

The sheriff squinted at him. "I don't think we've met."

Walker stuck his hand out. "Walker Black."

The sheriff shook his hand as she gave him the once-over that plainly said she was sizing him up. "You must be new in town."

"I am."

"You ever thought about applying to be a deputy?"

"Wasn't on my radar, no. Why, are you hiring?"

"Not at the moment. But you never know when a vacancy might come up." Sheriff Bull returned her attention to Charlotte. "I'll see you at your apartment in a few minutes, then."

"Except…" Charlotte glanced behind her. "I don't think Mrs. Merriweather will let me leave."

Sheriff Bull snorted. "It's not up to her. This is official business. Get the old bird over here, I'll talk to her."

Charlotte nodded and left the front desk.

Walker walked around the desk, positioning himself closer to the sheriff. "I don't know who the

Belmont brothers are, but do you think that's who ransacked the library yesterday?"

She narrowed her eyes again. "I haven't ruled it out. What do you think?"

He mulled it over, making a mental note to add the Belmont brothers to the possible suspect list. "Two break-ins in two days? I'm not much on coincidence."

She let out a sigh. "Neither am I. And I don't know if you've picked up on this, but things happen in this town sometimes that have…unusual reasons."

Did that mean the sheriff was wise to the supernatural side of things? He played dumb. "Not sure what you mean."

Her brows lifted. "I think you do. I might be human, but I'm not stupid."

That answered that. She knew. With that new information, he kept thinking out loud. "Means Charlotte could be the target." At least, that's what it meant to Walker. Whoever had broken into her apartment either knew she had the book or thought she did. And chances were excellent they'd found it. He'd need to contact Stillwell about that immediately. And have him dig for info on the Belmonts. The only upside was this break-in decreased the chances that Charlotte was working for the Collective.

"Maybe." The sheriff gave Walker a long look.

"But what would Charlotte have that's worth all the bother? She doesn't strike me as the type with a secret stash of jewels or cash. I don't disagree that Charlotte's being targeted, but I don't see how she fits in yet."

"I don't know." He wasn't about to reveal anything about the book to the sheriff. Just because she was wise to the supernatural business that went on in town, didn't mean she knew about the book or Charlotte being a witch. And that last bit was not his to reveal. He also got the feeling that the citizens of Everlasting understood there was some supernatural stuff happening in their town, but sort of gave it the side eye and let it be. The sheriff included. He didn't blame them, being human. "I was at her house last night for dinner. I didn't see anything valuable enough to warrant a break-in."

"You were there last night? And now you're here this morning. Where were you before you got here?"

He smiled, because he'd known that question was coming. "Went for a run, then Chickadee's for breakfast, then straight here. Easy to confirm."

She nodded. "All right."

Charlotte came back out with a fuming Millie. The woman's face was pinched into an expression of utter exasperation. "What's this about Charlotte needing to leave?"

Sheriff Bull planted her feet and puffed out her chest a little. "That's right. She's been the victim of a crime and I need her on the scene. You aren't going to stand in the way of the law, are you, Millie?"

Millie's pinched expression softened slightly. Very slightly. "No, of course not. But it does leave me in a bind. I'll be here all alone."

"Unless Judge Turnbury has left, he'll be the only other patron in the building," Walker pointed out. "I'm headed out myself."

Millie sniffed. "There could be an influx of patrons at any moment."

"I'll send a deputy over to keep you company. November's free." Sheriff Bull squeezed the radio on her shoulder and got hold of the deputy in question, giving him the command to hightail it to the library.

When she was done, she nodded at the three of them. "All right, let's go, we're wasting daylight. I'll see you over there."

Walker liked the sheriff. She said exactly what she meant. People like that made good allies. And even better sources of information. "Charlotte, you want to grab your coat while I bring the truck around?"

"Oh, right." She went into the back room of the library again.

He headed out to the parking lot and started up his truck, cranking on the heat to take the chill off. The sheriff drove past, giving him a wave. He waved back, then pulled the truck around to the front of the library.

Charlotte came out a few moments later, hands shoved deep into her coat pockets. Her gaze was a thousand miles away. She climbed in, put her seat belt on and stared through the windshield like she was on autopilot.

"You okay?"

It took a second, but she looked at him. "Someone broke into my apartment. Do you think this is about the book? It has to be. It's the only valuable thing in there. Besides Edgar Allan."

He wanted to hug her. Comfort her in some way. But she might not welcome it and she had enough to deal with. "Yes, probably, just like that's why the library was ransacked yesterday. They want that book."

"You know it's just an old book of magic, right? But the thing is, grimoires aren't exactly rare."

He eased off the brake and got them moving toward her place. "This one is. Rare and extremely dangerous. In the right hands. Which…" He glanced at her. "Yours are, apparently. It can be used to—"

"How do you know my hands are the right ones? Wait, how *do* you know about this book? And that I'm a witch?"

"I know about the book because I work for an organization whose mission is to protect the world from dark magic." The FOL wasn't going to like him sharing so much, but he didn't care about them right now. Just Charlotte. She was all that mattered in this moment. "And I know you're a witch because I'm a shifter and I can sense that you're not human. Just like you can probably sense I'm not either."

She frowned. "I didn't pick that up at all. What kind of shifter are you?"

"Leopard."

"That explains Edgar Allan's reaction to you."

Walker just nodded and let her process all the new information.

She spoke a minute later. "So you're not really an antiquer after all."

"No, I am. But I specialize in magical objects." He knew he needed to tell her he was a witch hunter, but now was not the right time. Not with all she was dealing with. Plus, that info might turn her against him. He liked Charlotte too much to lose her trust. He'd tell her, but at the right time. Besides all that, he couldn't help but feel like she needed someone on her side. Someone who could protect her from the Collective. "I recover those objects and turn them in to the organization, then they make sure the objects can never be used to hurt anyone again."

She seemed to think that over for a moment. "And how do you know that my hands are the right hands?"

"Because you said you can open the book. I assume you can see the spells on the pages, too?" He rounded the bend. No sign of the sheriff. The woman must have a lead foot.

"Yes. What does that mean?"

"That the book has chosen you. For the remainder of your life, no one else will be able to open it or read what's inside. You have become the book's keeper." Or she would, once she'd bonded with the book. Which he really hoped she hadn't done yet.

"That's…nuts."

"That's Middian's." He eased the heat back. "No one knows for sure how it got that way, but it's proven to be true for at least two centuries."

"The book is that old?"

"Yes. And it considers this town its home, which is why it showed up at the library. That's where it always shows up when the current owner passes. Oh, one more thing. The new keeper of the book is granted one wish, so be careful what you say around the book. Not that it matters now."

"Why's that?"

He made a face. "Because whoever broke into your apartment is most likely in possession of it."

"No, they're not."

He shot her a look. "Was your hiding place that good?"

"No, but that's not what I meant. The book isn't in my apartment."

"Then where is it?"

"It's in my tote bag. Back in the library."

It took everything in him not to let out a whoop of happiness. "Why did you bring it to work? I'm really glad you did, but why?"

"I don't know. I just felt…compelled to keep it with me. I guess I thought maybe I'd have time on my lunch break to look through it." She held a hand up. "Not that I'm going to try any of the spells or anything. I'm just a novice. That book is way more complicated than anything I can manage right now."

"You're a novice?" He found that hard to believe.

"Yep." She pointed left as they approached a four-way stop. "Turn left here. Wait. You've been to my apartment before. Sorry, the stress is getting to me."

"Completely understandable. And we are coming from a different direction so it's helpful." He made the left. "What were you saying about being a novice?"

"I only just found out I was a witch a couple months ago. The only spells I can do are pretty basic ones, except for the fire spell. I have yet to get that one right without causing a small inferno."

How was it possible that she was a new witch? "That's not what I thought at all."

"What did you think?"

"That you were one of the most powerful spell casters I'd come up against in a long time."

She gave him an odd look. "Why would you think that? The only magic I've done recently was definitely not aimed at you and didn't go that well anyway. Granted, it might have accidentally affected you, and if it did, I apologize. Stupid love spell." She sighed. "I'm supposed to be practicing, but my mentor only got back into town this week and I've kind of been slacking off. Plus cleaning up the library after it was vandalized wore me out."

"You cast a love spell? And you think it accidentally hit me?"

Her head spun toward him like it was on a swivel. "Calm down. I said it *might* have affected you. What are you so worried about? You're the one who kissed me. Of course, if that spell did hit you then, oh, never mind. Did you or did you not kiss me first?"

"That explains it."

"Explains what?"

"Magic. That explains it. Just magic gone wrong." He laughed, hearing the nerves in his own voice.

"That explains what?"

"I just thought…I was starting to have feelings for you."

She stared at him, wide-eyed. The tiniest bit of what looked like panic – or maybe it was horror – crept into her gaze. "You. Have feelings. For me."

He frowned. The Seaview apartments were just ahead, which was good, because he was ready for this conversation to be over. "After what happened in your kitchen? After the way you kissed me? You're telling me that none of that affected you."

She swallowed and stared at the cluster of patrol cars clogging up the lot. "My feelings are a little jumbled right now. And even if I was having feelings, which I'm not, I'd nip them in the bud because you're just passing through. And not even my type."

"Good to know."

"Look, if I led you to think there was something going on between us, or that something was possible between us, I'm sorry. Last night was just dinner. I thought you could tell me more about the book. That was all."

He angled the truck into a spot and turned the engine off.

She jumped out of the truck before he could say another word.

Chapter Ten

Charlotte was torn. She wanted to talk to Walker about as much as she didn't want to talk to Walker. He'd given her so much new information about the book and about him (a leopard shifter!) that it only made trying to focus on the task at hand – dealing with her home being violated – incredibly difficult. And right now, the best she could do was one thing at a time. So she tucked away everything he'd shared until some later date when the space in her head wasn't already so full.

Whenever that might be.

She trudged up the steps to her apartment, dreading what lay ahead. Sheriff Bull met her at the closed door. "Your apartment is currently an active crime scene, so while we're not concerned with you getting new prints on things, we don't want you moving anything until the whole place has been photographed."

Charlotte nodded. "Active crime scene. Got it." What a strange thing to hear said about the place you considered home. Everlasting wasn't exactly known for its high crime rate, either. The whole thing was just surreal.

"All right," the sheriff continued. "You and I are going to do a walk-through. It might be a little overwhelming, but I want you to tell me as best you can if anything's been taken."

"Okay. But I want to see my cat first. Where is he?"

"He's in the bathroom in the tub. Seems to be hiding out in there."

"Probably scared out of his mind."

"Might be," the sheriff said. "Or whoever broke in might have put him in there for safe keeping."

Charlotte huffed out a breath. "If you expect me to thank the burglars for their consideration, you're wrong."

Walker came up alongside Charlotte, but said nothing. Which she appreciated. She wasn't in the mood to be disagreed with.

The sheriff glanced at him, then back at Charlotte. "We'll head toward your cat then. See if maybe you can put him in a carrier or something, get him somewhere he'll be out of harm's way. Unless your landlord can get this lock fixed today, you're going to need to find another place to stay for a day or two."

Charlotte mulled that over. "I don't really have anywhere else to go. All of my friends have family in town for the Festival. Except for Sarah, who's allergic to cats, and Melody, who has a Great Dane. Not sure Edgar Allan is in any frame of mind to room with a dog the size of a donkey."

The sheriff made a face. "I'd say get a hotel room, but the town's booked up with tourists in for the Festival, too."

Walker put his hand on Charlotte's arm. "You and Edgar Allan can stay with me. I have the top-floor apartment at the Marlboro House. It's not much bigger than this place, but it has two bedrooms. Only one bath, but…" He shrugged. "I'm not a slob. And Edgar Allan will be safe there."

Charlotte frowned as she gave that some thought. She hardly knew Walker. But then, she had kissed him. Twice. Three times if you counted the quick goodbye kiss. And he knew she was a witch. Plus, he was a shifter, and although he was a visitor, there did seem to be a sort of family feeling among the supernaturals in town, which meant they were all inclined to help one another in times of need.

Maybe that's all Walker was doing. Extending a hand, the way family did. Although, if she was being truthful with herself, what she felt toward Walker was anything but sisterly affection. She wouldn't tell him that, and she refused to fall for someone who was only going to leave town and break her heart, but she liked him. More than she should. Maybe it was stress from the break-in. Was stress-induced infatuation a thing?

He looked at the sheriff. "I could probably replace the lock."

Charlotte frowned. "I don't want to stay here tonight. Not after this."

He stuck his hands in his jacket pocket. "Then maybe there's someone else you could bunk with for a day or two?"

"No," Charlotte said. "I'll take you up on your offer. If you really don't mind Edgar Allan staying with you."

Walker shook his head. "I don't. Not at all."

"Then thank you. It's very kind of you." And if he got out of hand, she'd zap him with an energy bolt. That was the first thing Lola had taught her and the one spell she could successfully cast every time.

"Good." The sheriff put her gloved hand on the doorknob. "Now that that's settled, let's get this walk-through over with so we know what we're dealing with here. Walker, why don't you come with us and help with the cat?"

Walker nodded. "I can take him down to the truck."

The sheriff shot him a look. "Charlotte's prints we don't mind, but you don't touch anything."

"My prints are already going to be in the apartment. I was here for dinner, remember?"

"Oh, right. We'd better take yours so we can rule them out. Okay, in we go." Sheriff Bull led them into the apartment. Two deputies were inside already. One was dusting for prints, the other was taking photos. The place was trashed.

Charlotte swallowed as she stopped at the edge of her living room. From here, she could see most of her small apartment. The kitchen cabinets were open, as was the cabinet on the TV stand. Books were pulled off the shelves, and in her bedroom, clothes from her dresser had been flung onto the bed. Her gut knotted up and her eyes went hot with the threat of tears.

Walker put his arm around her. "As soon as we're able, I'll help you straighten everything up."

"Thanks," she whispered.

"I know that's a small comfort looking at all this now, but the sheriff will figure out who did this." He gave her a little squeeze, then lowered his voice. "And we already know they didn't get what they came for."

"Right." She glanced at the sheriff. "I'll need to move a few things so I can put a bag together. Clothes and stuff like that. Supplies for Edgar Allan."

Sheriff Bull looked up from her conversation with one of the deputies. "Right, right. Try to disturb things as little as possible."

Charlotte nodded. "Okay. And I'll let you know if anything's missing, but right now, I'm going to get my stuff together."

The deputy gave her a sympathetic glance. "Sorry about all this, Charlotte."

"Thanks." She went into the bedroom. Walker followed. The room was just as much of a mess as the rest of the house. "Wow. Did they have to go through everything?"

The dresser drawers that hadn't been emptied were open and looked like they'd been stirred up. Bras and underwear spilled out of the top drawer like a lacy pastel wave. She grimaced. She wanted to shove them back in, but that would be moving stuff.

"You okay?"

"Yes. No." She groaned. "I don't think I can wear underwear that a stranger has fondled. Maybe not even after it's been washed."

"I…uh…" He looked away, his skin slightly flushed. Apparently discussing her underwear was more than the big, bad leopard shifter could handle.

It made her smile a little.

He took a few steps toward the closet, which looked like a bomb had gone off inside. "Do you have a suitcase I can get for you?"

She made herself stop smiling and answered

him. "Get Edgar Allan's carrier for me first. It's on the top shelf of the closet, far right. Or it was."

"I see it." He took it down while she went into the bathroom and peeked behind the shower curtain. Edgar Allan hissed then started forward to butt his head against her hand. "I know, baby, it's been a rough day, huh? I'm so glad you're okay."

Because if he hadn't been okay, if he'd been hurt…suddenly, the tears came. She scooped his big, warm body into her arms and leaned against the bathroom counter, burying her face in his orange fluff.

"Hey," Walker said softly. "You're okay, and he's okay, and that's what matters, right?"

She sniffed and nodded, picking her head up. "Yes. But it's the scariest thing that's ever happened to me. What if Edgar Allan had been hurt? What if I'd been home?"

"But he wasn't and you weren't." Walker brushed a strand of hair off her cheek. "And I'm very glad for that because then I would have to hunt them down and make them pay. Which I'm probably going to do anyway."

She smiled a little. "You haven't known me long enough to avenge me."

"I was talking about if they'd hurt my boy, Edgar Allan. Being that we're practically related and all."

The cat picked his head up and chirped at

Walker, making Charlotte laugh. "Edgar Allan, you silly thing." She scratched him under the chin. "I can't imagine how freaked out he was."

"Poor guy. I put the carrier on the bed. Let's get him in there, then I can take him down to the truck while you pack a bag."

"Perfect." She carried Edgar Allan out and tucked him into the carrier, which he went into without a fuss, further proof that the poor animal had had enough of his current situation. "I'll get another bag together with his food and a bowl and he'll need a litter box and—"

"Charlotte," Walker said. "I can do that. You get yourself sorted. I'll take care of all the cat stuff."

"You're sure?"

"I'm positive. Also, I'd like to remind you that I live at the Marlboro House. It's ten minutes away. In the same town. If we forget something, we'll come back for it or buy it."

"Okay, right. Thanks." She leaned in and kissed his cheek. "I really do appreciate this."

"Happy to do it." He picked up the carrier. "All right, Edgar Allan. I know I'm not your mother, but she'll be along shortly, I promise."

She watched him go as he took her cat down to his truck. Today was a horrible day, but it wasn't all bad. Not with Walker around.

WALKER PUT the carrier and a grocery bag of cat food he'd gathered in the kitchen onto the front seat. He locked the truck, then jogged back upstairs for the rest of the cat's things. Namely the jug of litter and the box it went in. Those could go in the bed of the truck.

The apartment door was open and Charlotte was standing in the small foyer, a large duffel bag slung over her shoulder, talking to the sheriff. "Nothing missing that I could see."

"You're sure?" the sheriff asked.

"As best I could tell, yes."

Walker stepped next to Charlotte. "I just need to grab the rest of Edgar Allan's stuff and we're ready to go."

She looked at him. "Thanks." She glanced at the sheriff again. "You'll let me know if you find out anything?"

The sheriff nodded. "I have your number."

Walker tipped his head toward the door as he spoke to Charlotte. "Go ahead to the truck if you want. I'll be right behind you."

"Okay. Thanks." She headed out.

He grabbed the litter and the litter box, then went down to the truck and put them in the bed. Charlotte was in the passenger's seat with the carrier on her lap. Her bag was at her feet. He got in, closed the door, and started the truck to get the heat going again. It wasn't freezing yet, but there was a chill in the air. "If you didn't find anything missing, that confirms whoever broke in was after the book."

"Right."

"You have more questions, don't you?"

She nodded. "I do."

"You want to ask them now?"

"Yes."

"Go ahead." He'd answer as truthfully as he could. She deserved that.

"What's this organization you work for?"

"The Fraternal Order of Light. FOL for short."

"And they hired you because you're a leopard shifter?"

"They didn't exactly hire me. When I was an infant, I was left on the doorstep of one of their agents. He adopted me, raised me as his own. Going to work for the FOL just seemed like the thing to do."

"Is it only men then? Fraternal seems very…manly."

"It was originally. But not these days."

"This man who adopted you, was he a shifter too?"

"No, he was human. But he did his best to teach me about who I really am."

"Are there other supernaturals that work for the FOL?"

"Yes. A lot, actually."

"And you just sensed that I was a witch?"

"The FOL knew there was a witch working at the library. We just didn't know who until I figured out it was you. But I do have a pretty good magical radar."

She looked at him as she hugged the carrier closer. "What kind of training did the FOL put you through?"

That was not going to be an easy question to answer honestly, and lying to her, with everything else going on, felt like a step in the wrong direction. Telling her the truth could send her running, and she was going to need his protection.

He made himself smile and did his best to answer factually, if not completely. "All kinds. Fighting techniques, tracking, weapons, magic, languages, runes, history. You name it, they taught it."

It seemed to satisfy her, but he was still happy to change the subject. "Do you want to go by the library before we head to my place? Maybe pick up the book?"

"That's probably not a bad idea. Millie won't like that I'm leaving again but she's just going to have to sit tight until I get back from setting Edgar Allan up at your place."

"You could stay at the library if you wanted. I can always take your stuff to the apartment.

Including Edgar Allan. But I'm sure he'd feel better if you were there to get him settled in."

"Yep, me too."

"Millie ought to give you the rest of the day off. Having your place broken into is stressful. To say the least."

"It's okay, I don't mind going back to work. The activity will help keep my mind off the break in. And the only other librarian is part time and today's one of his days off."

"Okay, if you're sure."

She slanted her eyes at him. "It's very nice of you to let me stay with you, and I really appreciate it, but I think I should say up front that there better not be any funny business. Not that I think that's why you offered. I just think I should say it. Also, since you know I'm a witch, it's worth telling you that I'm adept at conjuring bolts of magical electricity at will. I've been told they could stop a charging elephant, so a leopard should be no problem."

He smirked. "No funny business intended, I swear. But good to know about the magical electricity all the same."

A few minutes later, he pulled into the library parking lot. "I'll stay here with Edgar Allan. That way I can keep the heat on for him."

"Good." She hopped out, then stood there with the door ajar. "I won't be long. I'm just going to grab my tote bag, tell Millie I'll be back as soon as possible, then we can go to your place. Or should I drive my own car over there? Then you don't have to drive me back."

"I'm happy to drive you back. It's one less thing for you to worry about right now."

"Okay." She smiled a little. "Thanks."

She shut the door and went inside. He turned on the radio, finding something soft. Music was supposed to be soothing for animals and humans alike, and her cat was putting out some seriously unhappy vibes. Walker peered into the carrier. "You okay in there, buddy? I know it sucks, but you'll be out of there soon enough."

The cat's gold gaze locked onto Walker, and he meowed.

Walker shook his head. "I wish you could tell me who broke in." He sighed. He could get a sense of the animal's mood, what he liked and didn't, but actual communication wasn't possible. Cats, after all, couldn't talk. "Listen, I promise I'm not going to hurt your mother. I like her. And I can tell she's one of the good guys. I wasn't sure at first, but I have to trust my gut. So you have nothing to worry about there, okay?"

Another meow answered him.

Walker leaned over and stuck his fingers through the front grate of the carrier so he could scratch the cat's cheek. "Just do me a favor? If you hate my apartment, don't leave any *presents* in my shoes or anywhere else in the morning, cool? I'm just renting. It's not like I had a lot of say in the place."

Charlotte came out of the library, eyes wide in panic. Her steps were short and clipped, like she was on the verge of running.

Walker got out of the truck to meet her. "What's wrong?"

She shook her head, refusing to speak until she was closer. She was pale, her grip tight on the straps of the tote bag slung over her shoulder. "The book is gone."

Chapter Eleven

Charlotte crouched to let Edgar Allan out of his carrier and into Walker's small living room. "There you go, baby."

The cat stuck his head out, sniffed a few times, then cautiously walked forward to explore.

His food and water were already arranged on a tea towel in the narrow galley kitchen, and the litter box had been squeezed into the bathroom between the toilet and the vanity. Edgar Allan would find it. Cats were smart and he was no exception.

She straightened and repeated what she'd said in the car, because it was still settling in. "The book being gone is bad. Really bad."

"I agree." Walker rubbed a hand over his face. "We have to figure out who was in the library while we were gone."

"That's easy." She watched Edgar Allan for a

second longer. He jumped onto the couch, the only furniture in the living room besides a coffee table and the stand holding the television, turned around once and settled down. "Besides you, me, and Millie, there was Judge Turnbury – he comes in every morning to read the papers. And Deputy November, since Sheriff Bull sent him over. There were also a few other regulars there when I went in. So, no one who looked shady or like a criminal."

"What about people who might have come and gone while you weren't there?"

"I can ask Millie. I guarantee she'll know. No one escapes her scrutiny."

"Unless she's the one who stole the book."

Charlotte frowned. "Do you think that's possible? I mean, why would she? She thinks it's garbage, for one thing. She tossed it out after it showed up in the book return box. I only have it now because I went into the bin after it."

"Maybe for that reason alone. Maybe she's mad you got it out of the trash after she threw it away. She could have chucked it in the bin again."

"But she wouldn't have known it was in my tote bag."

His brows lifted. "Unless she regularly snoops through your stuff."

A soft growl escaped Charlotte before she could stop herself. "That would be so like her. Nosy woman. But I can check the garbage when I get back to the library. I'll see if I can tell who else was in while I was gone, too."

"Do you have security cameras? Maybe you could look through this morning's footage."

She laughed. "Security cameras in the library of Everlasting?"

"Yeah, forget I asked."

She glanced at Edgar Allan, who was now snoozing. "I guess there's nothing else for me to do here. I should get back. Millie's already in a mood about me being gone. The longer I'm away, the worse it'll get."

He swung his keys around his finger. "Are you still up to dinner tonight at Chickadee's when you get off?"

She rolled her lips in for a moment like she was thinking. "Could we maybe order in a pizza instead? It's Friday and with the tourists in town, the diner will be mobbed. I'd rather just stay in and crash after…everything."

"Sounds like a plan. That's what we'll do. Provided you know a place that delivers. Or I can pick it up." He opened the door that led to the small landing and the stairs. All three flights of them.

"Remo's delivers. They have subs too, if you don't want pizza."

"Nope, I'm good with pizza." He waited for her to go ahead of him, then locked the door and followed her down. "In fact, if you tell me what you like, I can order it so it gets here right after you do. You get off at seven, right?"

"Right. So I should be here about seven fifteen. I like pretty much anything but pepperoni."

"How about mushroom and sausage? And extra cheese?"

"I'm in. And climbing all these steps will help me burn off that extra cheese." She laughed. "Just let me know what I owe you and I'll give you my half when I get back."

"You're my guest. It's on me."

She looked over her shoulder at him. "Walker, you don't need to do that. I'm already invading your space with myself and my cat. I can handle my half."

"I know you can, but it's not allowed." He grinned. "Sorry, house rules, guests don't pay."

"Walker—"

"Nope," he cut her off. "End of discussion."

She put her hand on the door that led to the small parking lot. "I don't need charity."

He stopped in front of her, a little closer than was polite. "Good, because this isn't charity. I like you. I want to help you. And you should let me. I've gone up against the kind of people who want this book before. They're not nice. They won't give a second thought to hurting anyone who gets in their way."

"And yet, they put my cat in the bathroom when they ransacked my apartment."

"Whoever was working for them did that, because a real agent of the Collective wouldn't have cared one bit about what happened to Edgar Allan."

"You're scaring me a little."

He put his hand on the door frame. "Being afraid of them is smart. But I can and will protect you. I promise. You just have to help me find that book before they do."

"I will absolutely help you. But what if they find it first?"

He hesitated. "Let's just pray that doesn't happen. But there's sort of a built-in fail safe, provided the book doesn't decide whoever stole it is its new owner."

"What's that?"

"By midnight tonight, if the book still thinks you're its keeper, it'll either return itself to you, or return itself to the library. There's nothing in my files about this situation. If it returns itself to you, all you have to do is hand it over to me and I'll take care of the rest."

"And if midnight rolls around and it's not in my possession?"

He grimaced slightly. "Then I'm going to the library to find that book before the Collective does."

"The first time it showed up, it was in the return box, so we can start there."

"There's no *we*, Charlotte. I'm going alone. These people are dangerous."

She wiggled her fingers at him, letting the magical sparks of her one good power dance over her fingertips. "So am I."

WALKER DROPPED Charlotte at the library then headed to the Witch's Brew, a coffee shop in town that seemed aptly named for everything that was going on. It was a comfortable, homey place. He got a coffee and a cranberry scone and found a table by the window where he could keep an eye on the street while he texted with Stillwell.

Book is missing. The witch isn't involved. She's going to help me find it. He drank his coffee while he waited for Stillwell to reply. It was good coffee, dark roast. The scone wasn't bad either.

Stillwell responded a minute later. *Still need the witch.*

This wasn't a battle to be fought via text, but Walker *would* fight it. There was no way he was bringing Charlotte in and subjecting her to life confined to the FOL cells. *Need intel on Mildred Merriweather. Also Belmont brothers. No first names yet.*

Walker only had a single corner of his scone left

by the time Stillwell answered. Wasn't much of an answer, just a link to a downloadable file and the words, *Nothing on Belmont yet*.

The man might not be much of a conversation-alist, but he was fast with the intel. Walker clicked the link and started the download. While he waited for it to finish, he ate the last of his scone. Then he opened the file and started reading.

Mildred Merriweather was far more interesting than he would have imagined. She'd been quite the activist in college and had been arrested twice for protesting. Both times were for environmental issues. He stared at his screen. Millie had been a trou-blemaker.

Was she still?

He read on, delving into the financials Stillwell had provided. The woman lived modestly and had a small savings, but not much in the way of retire-ment. And she had a hefty amount of debt. How much money would it take for her to steal a book from the library she guarded so fiercely? According to Charlotte, Millie had thrown the book out initially. Maybe that had been her plan. Throw it out, then retrieve it from the trash later and sell it to her contact at the Collective.

Sometimes the Collective hired a supernatural to do their retrievals, because they were better at controlling the object in question, but there was nothing in Millie's file to indicate that she was anything other than human. But it wouldn't be that unusual if the Collective had hired her. She was the head librarian at the library the book considered home. And most people in town seemed to know the supernatural was alive and well in Everlasting.

Plus, the Collective was a mix of supernaturals and humans who'd had their eyes opened. Much like the FOL.

That made Walker wonder if Millie might know Charlotte was a witch. Millie knew a lot of other things about Charlotte. Where she lived. And what time she left for work. Would Millie have had time to toss Charlotte's place before arriving at the library herself? He'd have to ask Charlotte if Millie had been late.

But Charlotte's apartment was small. And the book was large enough that there were only so many places to hide it. He could have gone through her place in ten minutes if he'd been trying to find the book. And he wouldn't have left a spot untouched.

He drained his coffee. Millie was looking more and more like a person of interest. He stared out the window, watching the street bustling with tourists in town for the Festival. If Millie had the book, that meant it was still in the library. Unless she had already handed it off to the Collective, or was about to.

Jumping to his feet, he threw a five on the table and tucked his phone in his pocket. He had to get back to the library and tell Charlotte what he suspected. If the book was still in the library, they'd find it.

And if it wasn't, it might be time for him to have an up-close-and-personal discussion with Mildred about things much, much worse than late fees.

Chapter Twelve

"Hey."

Charlotte jumped and let out a little shriek that she sucked back in as soon as it began. Walker was behind her in the middle of the Social Sciences section. She gave him a swat on the arm. "You scared the pants off me."

He smirked and his gaze shifted downward. "Clearly, I did not."

"You know what I mean." She shoved the book she was holding onto the shelf where it belonged, then crossed her arms. Her heart was pounding from being startled. "You're lucky I didn't zap you. What's up?"

He looked over her shoulder for a second. "I think Millie's our thief."

"No. Get out. Really?" Charlotte checked

behind her too, even though Walker had just done that. "Why do you think that?"

"First, where is she?"

"It's the children's story hour. She's reading The Great Cat Sled Race to the local homeschoolers group and a few tourist kids."

"Good." He explained why he thought Millie had stolen the book, but Charlotte got the feeling he might not be telling her everything he'd learned about the head librarian, just enough to convince Charlotte of the woman's potential guilt. Which was fine. It was probably good she didn't know the deep, dark parts seeing as how she had to work with the woman. Better to keep her innocence that way, too. Or what was left of it.

He finished, and she considered everything he'd just told her. "So what now? We look for the book?"

"Yes. It should still be in the building unless Millie left."

"She didn't."

"Any chance she might have handed it off to someone?"

"I don't know. I have no idea what she did while I was gone."

"Then we need to be sure the book isn't here first." He rubbed the back of his neck. "How much longer is children's hour?"

Charlotte looked at her watch. "Twenty minutes

or so. More if the kids ask questions, but it just started. It's also not actually an hour."

"Where's her office? Where does she keep her things?"

"It's in the back, but it's more of a general work-space, although she uses it the most. We keep our personal items in the marked cubbies in the break room."

"Which is where?"

She narrowed her eyes. "Do you really intend to snoop through her things?"

"It's not snooping, it's recovering stolen property. Your stolen property. Which also happens to be a very dangerous book, in case you've forgotten."

"I haven't." She sighed. "I guess that means I'm on lookout?"

"That would be helpful."

"Head toward the back of the library. Break room is the first door on the left, office is the second one next to it." She scrunched up her nose. "And it's probably locked."

"I won't need a key unless it's an electronic lock."

"We're not that sophisticated."

"Then I can pick it. Keep your phone handy and my number pulled up. If she heads back that way, text me immediately."

"Okay. I'd say be careful, but the worst Millie can do to you is call the police." Charlotte put her hand to her mouth. "Hey, I just remembered. Deputy November is still here. The sheriff told him to hang out until we close. She thought it might make me feel better I guess."

"Are you sure? I didn't see him when I came in."

"He went out to get lunch, but he'll be back soon."

"Can you keep him out of my way when he returns?"

"Sure, I can manage that."

Walker smiled. "Don't worry, I'll be fast." He started toward the back of the library, then hesitated. "Find out from November who was in here while I was gone and if Millie spent any length of time with anyone or if anyone picked up a package from her. That will help a lot."

The library's door swished open.

Charlotte glanced to see who it was, then waved at Walker. "Go, that's Deputy November coming back now."

But Walker was already gone.

She put on a pleasant smile. Something in between nice-to-see-you and yes-I'm-doing-all-right-even-though-my-apartment-was-broken-into. It was a delicate balance.

Deputy November missed the subtly. "Hey, Charlotte, how you holding up?"

"I'm doing fine, thank you." She glanced at the takeout bag in his hand. He was going to want to use the break room. She couldn't let him do that. Not until she was sure Walker was out of there. "Hey, was the library busy while I was gone? I'd hate to think I missed anyone I'd reserved a book for."

He leaned against the counter, jangling his gun belt. He kind of stared off into space like he was thinking. "Ellen Dormand came in. Used one of the computers. Brent Kowalski dropped off a bunch of books his kids had checked out. Judge Turnbury finished his morning paper and left. Offered to get me a cup of coffee, but I told him there was coffee in the break room."

"That was nice of him. Anyone else?"

November rapped his fingers on the counter. "Oh. The Broadmoor sisters were in. They looked through a few cookbooks, copied a few recipes on the Xerox over there. Millie had to give them change for a dollar because neither one of them had dimes for the machine. That's about it, though."

"Okay, thanks." She snuck a peek toward the back. Still no sign of Walker.

"Sure thing. Guess I'll go eat."

She had to stall. "Hey, um, did you get that lunch from the diner?"

"No, I got it from Subs-n-More."

"Oh. I was wondering if you knew the soup today at Chickadee's. I was kind of in the mood for soup." She shrugged. "Comfort food. You know how it is."

"It's navy bean," Walker answered as he strolled up to the counter. "Saw it on the board when I had breakfast there. I'll go get you some if you want."

She exhaled in relief. "I might take you up on that."

Walker nodded at November. "Nice of you to hang out."

The deputy nodded back. "Protect and serve, that's what we do."

Walker pointed at the bag in his hands. "Hard to do on an empty stomach."

November laughed. "Just going to remedy that." He glanced at Charlotte. "You need me, just holler."

"Will do. Thanks." She held her smile until he rounded the corner toward the break room. Then she looked at Walker. "Well?"

"Nothing. It's not in her office or with her things. She either handed it off, stashed it some-where else, or she's not our thief."

Charlotte groaned. "November told me who was in the library while I was gone. No one I'd consider a suspect."

"Tell me."

She ran down the list of patrons November had given her. "None of those people seem likely to be involved in this. The Broadmoor sisters are sweet little old ladies who spend most of their time baking, and right now, they're prepping for the Cranberry Festival baking contest next weekend, so I don't think they're all that interested in much else. Judge Turnbury is, well, you've seen him."

Walker nodded. "He's not the heartiest of souls, is he?"

"Not since he retired and his wife died. I dread the day he doesn't show up at that front door." She shook her head, not wanting to think about the inevitable. "Brent Kowalski works at the hardware store. His wife is a nurse at the hospital and works some long shifts so he's almost like a single parent at times. And Ellen Dormand is a divorcee looking for love. She comes in here to use the computer to access her dating sites." Charlotte laughed. "She's actually had a few of her dates here, for that matter."

Walker blew out a breath. "You're right, none of them *sound* like they could be involved in this."

She squinted at him. "But you're going to check them out anyway."

He nodded. "I can't leave a stone unturned."

"And what about the book?"

He looked in the opposite direction toward where Millie was currently occupied with the kids and story time. "What kind of car does Ms. Merri-weather drive?"

"Why?"

"I have my reasons."

She narrowed her eyes. "You think she slipped out and put the book in there, don't you?"

"She could have. There is a back door. And you told me she parks back there."

"You really think breaking into her car is the right thing to do?"

"I'm not going to break into it. Just walk around it." He shrugged like it was the most innocent thing in the world. "Look inside."

Charlotte's brows lifted. "And if you see something that looks like the book?"

"Then I might break into it."

She shook her head. "You can't do that in broad daylight. If she has it, we'll confront her about it."

"At least tell me which of the cars out there is hers. I'll just take a peek."

"Her car is the Kia sedan, and it's the only car parked behind the library. That's all there's room for back there." She made air quotes. "Officially."

He smirked. "Thank you. I'll text you if I find anything, but I'm going to head out after I check her car and do some more recon. Unless you do want that soup?"

"No, I brought my lunch. Listen, you can't just—"

"You have a good day, then." He pointed a finger gun at her like he was that cool. Which he kind of was. "See you at Chickadee's for dinner."

"Walker," she hissed. But there was no stopping

him. He strolled out of the library with purpose, but Charlotte was scared he was going to get caught. As untested as her magic was, she muttered the little protection spell Lola had taught her and hoped it would be enough to keep him from ending up in jail.

Chapter Thirteen

No book in the car, Walker texted from the counter of Chickadee's. He hoped the text would be enough to keep Charlotte from worrying too much. The steam from his bowl of navy bean soup fogged the bottom of his phone screen. He wiped the glass off on his shirt sleeve, set the phone aside, and dug into the soup. It was really good. He'd have to get some and take it back to the apartment so Charlotte could have it later.

It was sweet that she was concerned, but he was more than capable of taking care of himself. He had been for many years and had done so against foes a lot more dangerous than Millie Merriweather. Actually, he didn't consider Millie dangerous at all. Humans generally weren't.

Now, the Collective agent who was her contact, whoever that was, posed a more serious threat. Most of them were highly trained operatives who would stop at nothing to further their cause. That person's identity remained to be discovered. And that bothered him. Not knowing who he was up against made his job harder.

Betsy stopped by to top off his coffee. "How's the soup?"

He swallowed the mouthful he'd just taken. "Perfect. I'll take an order to go."

"You got it. How about another biscuit? I'll get you another biscuit."

Being a regular had its perks.

His phone screen came to life with Charlotte's reply. *Did you break into her car or just look?*

Just look, he texted back. *Happy?*

Yes. Then on a new line she added, *Unless you're going to search her house too.*

He'd already decided that was his next step, but he knew Charlotte wouldn't be thrilled about it. There were no other options, though. Millie was at work until seven, so he'd have plenty of time to go through her home to see if he could find anything that might tie her to the Collective. *I don't have any other choice.*

Her answer was a sad face emoji and the words, *I don't like it, but be careful.*

I will. I always am. He almost added a heart emoji, then stopped himself. Where had that come from? He wasn't in love with Charlotte. Love took a long time. And love wasn't in the cards for an FOL agent. He stared at his phone, thinking about the past couple of days. He did like her an awful lot, though. He smiled. Hard not to when thinking about her. Could that be because of her poorly cast love spell? Maybe. But what he was feeling seemed very real.

Betsy came back with a small plate holding two steaming biscuits and a pile of foil-wrapped butter pats. "Here you go, fresh out of the oven. Take out order is coming up."

"Thank you." Hot biscuits definitely made the day a little brighter. Then his phone lit up with another text from Charlotte.

I have an idea. Are you willing to recruit a little outside help?

He put down the butter and answered her. *Outside help from who?*

Another witch. My mentor.

He stared at the screen. Having Charlotte's help was already pushing the boundaries of what the FOL considered SOP. But sometimes getting the job done meant ignoring the standard operating procedure.

Adding another witch to the mix, however, that might be a bridge too far. For Stillwell. Not for Walker. Not when Charlotte might be in danger. So this was going to have to be one of those things Stillwell didn't find out about.

Walker tapped his screen to respond. *Sure. Set it up. Just tell me when.*

Will do.

He was digging into a slice of cranberry apple pie when she texted again.

Seven thirty at her house. I'll drive. Good?

Good, Walker responded. That would give him ample time to swing by Millie's place and see if she'd been dumb enough to leave anything incriminating lying around.

———

NERVOUS ENERGY DANCED over Charlotte's skin as she parked in front of Lola Honeycutt's grand old Victorian. Lola had all the lights on, making the place twinkle like the centerpiece of a Christmas village. And while it wasn't a big house, Lola kept it in pristine condition. This was the first time the house hadn't been on the Cranberry Festival tour of homes in a long time, but Lola had said she was just too busy this year. Charlotte hoped to have a house like it someday, although there were days when that dream seemed further and further away.

"Here we are." She and Walker got out of the car. She'd barely had time to get to his place and change before they'd left again, but the rush worth it. She hadn't seen her mentor since she'd returned from her trip.

He stared up at the place. "Nice house."

"Very nice. I'd love to have a place like this."

He put his hands on his hips. "What did you say your mentor does? Besides being a witch."

"She teaches at the college and she's written a few books."

Walker grunted something. Then added, "I can't wait to meet her."

Thankfully, there was no sarcasm or derision in his voice. He sounded genuinely curious.

That didn't stop Charlotte's stomach from tying itself in a knot as they walked to the front door. She kept reminding herself that Walker wasn't her boyfriend and it didn't really matter what Lola thought of him. Sure, it did a *little*. Lola might not help them if she thought Walker wasn't on the up and up, but Charlotte doubted he'd be anything but his usual charming self.

Lola opened the door as they stepped onto the porch. "Hello, Charlotte." She stuck her hand out. "And you must be Walker."

"I am." He shook her hand. "It's a pleasure to meet you, Ms. Honeycutt."

Lola's eyes widened as their hands touched. "You're a…" Her shocked expression turned into a guarded smile as she dropped his hand. "You're a shifter."

He nodded. "Feline, yes, ma'am, I am. I hope you're not allergic to cats."

Lola laughed. "No, thankfully. But Charlotte didn't mention that."

"No? Well, Charlotte told me about you. All very good things."

She stepped back to let them in. "They'd better be. She doesn't want me to turn her into a toad."

Walker's mouth opened in a very uncertain way.

Lola laughed. "Just kidding. We don't really do that." She winked at Charlotte. "At least not to our sister witches."

Walker managed a smile then, but a little apprehension remained in his eyes. Charlotte figured that was healthy around Lola. The woman was extraordinarily powerful. She was also, to Charlotte's eyes, beautiful in an unconventional way. Her thick, black hair and big dark eyes added gravity to her tall, slender frame. She accented those eyes with smoky makeup and arched brows maintained to the point of perfection.

Lola shut the door behind them, then led them into the living room. Her home was just as beautiful on the inside as it was outside. Every room held expensive antiques and lovely fabrics, but still maintained a welcoming vibe. And to Charlotte's eyes, the house also had a slight witchy feeling to it. Maybe it was the occasional crystal on a side table, or the apothecary jars that dotted the shelves, or the titles of some of the books on those shelves.

Then again, maybe Charlotte only noticed those things because she was a witch too. To the uninitiated, all of that might just blend into the background.

Lola stopped halfway into the room. "Can I get you something to drink?"

Charlotte shook her head. "I'm fine. Walker?"

He held up a hand. "Thank you, but I'm good. We're going to Chickadee's for dinner after we leave here. Thank you for seeing us on such short notice, by the way."

Lola took a seat on one of the twin couches that made up the room's seating area. "Charlotte is always welcome in my home."

Charlotte almost snorted. Lola's way of letting Walker know he was the outsider wasn't really that subtle. Charlotte sat, patting the spot beside her to get Walker to join her. "Still nice of you. Especially because I know you've been traveling."

"Vacation?" Walker settled onto the couch, but didn't lean back. Like he wanted to be ready to move on a moment's notice.

"Work," Lola answered. "I was giving a lecture at the Archaic Studies group in Boston. Nice people. Bought every book I had at the signing." She clasped her hands and rested them in her lap. "Now, what can I help you two with? Charlotte didn't want to tell me much over the phone. Very mysterious. And I'm a sucker for a good mystery."

Charlotte took a breath. "I found a book. Or maybe it found me. Either way, it showed up at the library – someone put it in the book return box. Millie threw it away because it looked so ratty and the pages were glued together, but I rescued it and took it home."

"And let me guess," Lola said. "When you got it home, you found out the pages weren't actually glued together. And it wasn't so ratty after all."

"You know the book?" Charlotte asked.

"Middian's?" Lola shrugged. "Most of the higher-level witches in town know about it. Mostly because we've been waiting to see who would end up with it, for one. Mena Peabody, who is my mentor, was sure it would find its way to me, but I told her it would go to someone younger." She smiled broadly. "I see I was right. I'm not surprised it chose you, Charlotte. You have the potential to be one of the greatest witches New England has ever known."

Charlotte wasn't so sure about that, but the compliment was flattering all the same. "Thank you."

Lola lifted her clasped hands to her heart. "And just think. I knew you when."

Charlotte laughed. "I'm not there yet."

Lola leaned forward. "You haven't bound yourself to the book yet, have you? That will make turning it in far more difficult."

"Bound myself? Turning it in?" Charlotte rubbed her temple. "Back up. How would I bind myself to the book? And where would I turn it in to?"

"The binding is simple, really. Three drops of blood straight onto the pages. The ritual should be the first page the book opens to on its own. Have you seen it?"

"I haven't really gotten that far."

"Good." Lola leaned back. "Say, do you think I could come over and have a look at it? I've always wanted to see it for myself. Though, as I mentioned, you'll be expected to turn the book over."

Walker cleared his throat. "Turn it over to who?"

Lola's brows went skyward. "That book is very powerful and very dangerous. The witches of this town made a pact that whomever came into possession of the book would voluntarily turn it over to the coven to put into magical suspension."

Walker finally sat back. "Didn't work the last time, did it?"

Lola's eyes lit with an unhappy gleam. "If you're referring to Flora Mae—"

"I am."

"We tried everything to get her to turn over the book. She refused. We eventually revoked her membership in the coven. Before she moved, she used the book to hex the entire town with a dreadful flu that hospitalized a hundred and seventeen people."

"Your pact didn't do much good."

Lola sat up a little straighter. "The pact came about because of Flora Mae."

Charlotte put her hand on Walker's leg. "I haven't agreed to it yet, by the way."

Lola raised her brows. "But you will when you're initiated."

Walker glanced at Charlotte. "I don't think it matters now."

"Probably not," Charlotte agreed.

"Of course it matters," Lola said. "Why wouldn't it?"

Walker sighed and held his hand out as if to indicate Charlotte should be the one to explain.

So she did. "Because the book was stolen from me this morning. In fact, they broke into my apartment looking for it. That's why we're here. To see if there's anything you can do to help us recover it."

Lola sucked in a breath. "You weren't home, were you?"

"No. Thankfully."

"Is Edgar Allan okay?"

Charlotte smiled with the relief of being able to answer, "He is. Thanks for asking."

"That's good. But still, having your apartment

broken into is an utter violation." Lola's expression darkened and she sat very still for a few long seconds. Then she muttered a curse. The profane kind, as opposed to the witchy variety. "I should call the coven."

"No," Walker said. "We don't know who we can trust."

Lola's eyes narrowed. "Obviously, you can trust me."

"Charlotte trusts you. And I trust her." He smiled at Charlotte.

Lola shifted in her seat, slightly indignant if Charlotte was reading her right. "And you trust him, Charlotte?"

"Yes." She did. He'd given her no reason not to.

Lola's brows lifted. "Despite what he is?"

Charlotte frowned. "What do you mean?"

Beside her, Walker stiffened. "She has nothing to fear from me."

"You're keeping secrets, Mr. Black. And now that I know Charlotte's been put in a path of danger, I can't abide that. You need to tell her the truth about who you are. Or I will. I won't have one of my novice witches be hurt in whatever game you're playing."

"I'm not playing a game," Walker said. He glanced at Charlotte and took her hand. "I was going to tell you, I was. It's just not the kind of thing you can randomly drop into a conversation."

Charlotte tilted her head. "Tell me what?" She looked at Lola. "One of you needs to explain what's going on. Now."

Lola pointed one long, graceful finger at Walker. "This man you brought into my house? He's not exactly the kind of company people like us should be keeping."

The muscles in Walker's jaw tensed. "That's not true."

Charlotte could only shake her head. "I still don't know what you mean. Is it because he's one of the uninitiated?" She looked at Walker. "What are you?"

The soft glow of anger lit his beautiful eyes. The feline beast inside him. "I'm—"

"He's a hunter," Lola announced. Her mouth firmed into a hard line.

"A hunter?" Panic settled over Charlotte. Lola was upset and Charlotte didn't understand why. "I mean, I love animals as much as the next person, more really, but he's a shifter. Hunting is probably a big part of being that kind of—"

"A *witch* hunter," Lola snarled.

Charlotte blinked once, then laughed, but her laughter died out a second later. "Wait, are those actually real?" She looked at Walker. "Tell me you don't know what she's talking about."

He growled softly. "I do. And she's right."

Chapter Fourteen

Charlotte's horrified expression nearly undid Walker. She pulled her hand away.

Walker let it go. Reluctantly. "I can explain. And I was going to. It's just not the easiest thing to tell a witch you've been trained to hunt those of her kind who stray. Especially when that witch is…" *Becoming more than a friend. And is such a good kisser.* "Is you. I'm sorry I didn't say anything sooner, but I promise you, I absolutely was going to tell you and I am *not* here to hurt you or any other innocent witches."

"You swear that?"

"On my life. I don't hunt the innocent."

"Then why are you here?" Lola asked.

"Because," he said, "a witch hunter is who the Fraternal Order of Light sends when there's a case that involves a witch. I've come up against some that were pretty bad business. Clearly, you two are

153

nothing like that." Although he had his reservations about Lola. She was incredibly powerful, he could sense that. And the fact that she knew about the book but didn't want it for herself was curious. Maybe this job was making him see shadows where there weren't any, but if it turned out she was using Charlotte to get to the book…the very idea made him see red.

"No," Lola said. "We're nothing like that. Neither are any of the other witches in town."

Walker shot her a challenging stare. "Really? You don't think there's a single other witch in this town that might want that book for themselves? Because someone stole it out of Charlotte's bag this morning. Right after her apartment was ransacked in another attempt to find it. And two nights before that, the library had been broken into and torn apart. Someone took that book, and since only a witch can use it, the pool of suspects is pretty shallow."

Lola stared at him for a second, then relented. "Not every witch in town is a member of the coven, but those who are would never do such a thing. I can vouch for that. I told you, they've all signed the pact agreeing to turn the book over."

He snorted. "So they signed a piece of paper. What's to keep them from making off with the book anyway?"

She gave him a rather condescending look. "It's

not just any pact. It's a witch's pact. Signed in blood. Breaking it means you'd be marked."

"Marked how?" Walker asked. "Magically?"

"Yes. The unfaithful witch's aura would bear the black scar of betrayal. She would be forever branded. Shunned by the magical community."

He looked at Charlotte. "Can you see auras?"

"No. That's a little advanced for me."

He turned back to Lola. "I'm guessing you can see them. Is that how you knew what I was?"

She nodded. "That and when you shook my hand. Charlotte, you had to have felt the sharp jab of dark energy that comes off him? That's the bite of a witch hunter's touch. Unless, you two haven't had any contact."

"No," Charlotte said. "We have. But I didn't notice anything."

Lola looked concerned. Then she shifted back to Walker. "Have you put some sort of hex on her to keep her from noticing?"

"No, I swear it. Although I initially thought she'd put some kind of spell on me…"

"You did?" Charlotte asked. "Why would you think that?"

"I told you," he said. He lowered his voice. "Because of the way I was feeling around you."

"Oh. Right. That." Charlotte frowned. "So why can't I feel this dark energy?" She laid her hand over top of his, then took it off again. "Nope. Nothing. Why is that, Lola?"

The woman shook her head. "Perhaps you're too much of a novice yet. Clearly, we need to step up your lessons."

Walker leaned forward, putting his elbows on his knees. "Look, the book is missing. And this is serious. You know who I am, I know who you are, let's work together to find it. That's why Charlotte asked if we could speak with you. She thinks you can help us. Can you? Will you?"

Lola glanced at Charlotte before answering him. "I can. But I won't. Not until you swear you won't hurt any of the coven members, just like you swore you wouldn't hurt Charlotte."

He sat back, the muscles in his jaw flexing. "I can promise no harm to anyone who's innocent. But if one of them is the thief? Or if one of them is working with the Collective? Then all bets are off, because I am here to recover that book and if possible, take into custody the Collective agent trying to attain it. And I will. No matter what it takes. I've never failed a mission yet. But trust me, you wouldn't want that person in your coven anyway."

When neither woman spoke, he continued. "I realize it's not fun to think that someone you know has been living a double life. That they aren't the person you thought they were. But this goes beyond Everlasting. Beyond whatever friendships you might have, or your perceived loyalty to the coven. This is about protecting mankind as a whole. That book is dangerous and needs to be dealt with. End of story."

Lola studied the amethyst ring on her right hand. "I feel like I'm betraying my circle by joining forces with you."

"I will promise you this. Help me, and I will be in your debt. If you ever need anything, you can call on me. That has to be worth something."

Lola sighed and threw up her hands. "Fine. I'll do what I can. But you have to be honest with me and Charlotte from here on out. And if you hurt Charlotte in any way, we are done, hunter. And you will be in a world of trouble. Do you understand me?"

"I do."

She let out another reluctant breath. "What do you need me to do?"

At last they were getting somewhere. "Call a coven meeting. Make it mandatory if you have to, but get everyone there. Check their auras, but don't say anything about the book. Then let me know what you find out. In the meantime, I'll be keeping an eye on the woman I already suspect."

"And that person is?" Lola waited expectantly.

"Millie Merriweather," Charlotte replied.

Lola's eyes widened. "Millie? The librarian?" She laughed. "You're wasting your time there. The woman's not even a witch. What on earth would make you think she's involved?"

Charlotte shrugged. "She was there at all the right times. She had access. We just don't know who she could be working with."

Lola smirked. "So you suspect her and think she has an accomplice?"

"Well, since she's not a witch, she wouldn't be able to use the book herself."

"I suppose that's true. Still, it seems like a real stretch." Lola stood. "Well, if I'm calling a coven meeting, I have work to do. And you two need to eat your dinner. I'll be in touch through Charlotte."

"Thank you. I appreciate your help." Walker got to his feet, Charlotte right behind him.

Lola pursed her lips. "Make no mistake, hunter, I'm doing this for the greater good. And because Charlotte's been caught up in all this. Not to help you."

He snorted. "I get it. But whatever your reasons, the end result will be the same and that's what matters to me. If we turn up anything, I'll make sure Charlotte keeps you in the loop."

"I expect nothing less." Lola walked them to the door, then offered them both a strange smile. "Happy hunting."

CHARLOTTE DIDN'T SAY a word to Walker for the first couple minutes they were in the car. She figured he'd earned that uncomfortable silence. She was mad. But she also understood why he might not have wanted to tell her exactly who he was.

And outside of holding that information back, which was pretty significant, he'd done nothing else for her to be upset about. He'd opened his apartment to her and Edgar Allan, after all, and that wasn't something everyone would have done. Unless that was part of his plan to keep her close so he could turn her over to his boss. But he wouldn't do that, would he?

She snuck a peek at him as she drove them to the diner. He looked miserable. Deeply, repentantly miserable. Nothing about him seemed like he was a man out to double cross her. She believed that with every instinct she had. Just looking at him it was plain to see he was obviously sorry about the whole thing.

She started to speak, but then he broke the silence before she could get a word out.

"I really am sorry, Charlotte. I knew I had to tell you, but I was sure it would make you uncomfortable around me, or maybe suspicious of me, and with everything that's going on, I was afraid you'd bolt. I didn't want to not be around you to protect you."

"You think I need protecting?"

159

"Yes, I do."

That was sweet. She couldn't remember anyone ever expressing a desire to protect her before. Didn't mean she wasn't still a little angry with him. "I pretty much understand why you didn't tell me. I'm not wicked happy about it, but I get it."

"You do?"

She kept her hands on the wheel and her eyes mostly on the road. "Yes."

He let out a sigh of relief. "I couldn't come up with a single scenario in which you didn't freak out, and with you staying in the spare room…" He shoved a hand through his hair. "I did not mean to upset you. And I meant what I said. I am not here to hurt you."

"I believe you."

"Thank you." He relaxed with a sigh, leaning back into the seat. A few moments passed before he spoke again. "Were you not talking to me when we first got in the car because you were upset?"

"Yes. And just because I'm talking to you now doesn't mean I'm not still upset." The diner was only five more minutes down the road. She'd probably stay reasonably mad through dinner at least.

He sighed. "Fair enough."

But she wasn't done talking things out. "If I'd felt something when we touched the first time, you would have had to explain. Or lie."

"I know. And I really didn't want to lie."

"You should have told me right away."

"You're right. I should have. But I also didn't know if you were working for the Collective or not. I don't typically walk up to potential opponents and introduce myself and spell out my mission. That's how you get dead in my line of work."

She hadn't thought about that. Her anger dialed back to mostly just miffed. "I suppose that's true."

He was giving her puppy dog eyes, she could see that much in her peripheral vision. "Forgive me?"

She wasn't *that* easily swayed. "I'm thinking about it."

"I'm buying dinner."

"Yeah, you are." She shot him a quick look. "What does it mean that you're a witch hunter? Have you actually hunted witches down?"

"You really want to know this stuff?"

"Yes, I do. I need to know what kind of person you are. And what it is you really do, since it's not antiquing like you told me."

"I do some antiquing, that wasn't a total lie."

"Sure, if the objects are old and magical. Right?"

He lifted one shoulder. "Right. Well, sometimes they're not old, just magical. It's part of my job as an FOL recovery agent."

"Which stands for what again?"

"Fraternal Order of Light. They really are the good guys. They exist to balance the dark forces at work in the world. Which is why I'm here after this book."

Sounded like a worthwhile operation. "What else have you recovered?"

"One of the three rings of the Zennet trilogy."

"Never heard of it."

"That would be because I confiscated one of the rings before it could be turned on and a portal to the demon realm opened. You're welcome, by the way. Humanity would have ceased to exist if that had happened."

She pulled into Chickadee's parking lot. "Really?"

"Really."

"Wow." She shifted the car into park and turned off the engine. Maybe she was being too hard on him. Walker really wasn't one of the bad guys. Dark magic was incredibly dangerous. "You still haven't answered my other question. Have you hunted down witches?"

"Yes. But only the bad ones."

"Have you ever…killed any?"

His hesitation was answer enough. "Yes. One. But it was in self-defense. Usually I take them into custody and turn them over to the FOL." His gaze darkened and drifted to a faraway place. "I had no choice. She would have killed me. Tried. Hard. Almost succeeded."

"What did she do?"

"Immobilized me with a spell, then sent a bolt of lightning through me. Apparently that's big with witches."

She cringed, thinking about how she'd threatened to do that to him. "That had to hurt."

"Like you can't imagine. But I survived." He smiled but it didn't remove the pain in his eyes.

"I'm glad. I really am." They could talk more over dinner. Especially because she wasn't mad anymore. She couldn't be. He was just doing his job. "Come on, let's eat."

They went inside and got a table. Most of the dinner rush was finishing up and they snagged the back booth again.

Their server, a short redhead with the name Macy on her badge, brought them waters. "Evening. Special tonight is meat loaf. Anything else to drink besides the water?"

"Coffee," Walker said. "What about you, Charlotte?"

It had been a long day. "Chocolate milk shake. And I'll have the special. I don't need to look at the menu."

Walker's smile brightened his whole face this time. "Make that two."

"Two specials, two chocolate milk shakes?" Macy asked.

He nodded. "Yep."

"All right." Macy left.

He leaned forward. "I had a look around Millie's house today."

Charlotte clapped her hands over her ears. "I'm not sure I should be hearing this."

"I didn't find anything, if that makes you feel better."

She put her hands down. The whir of the milk shake machine filled the diner. "I guess. But how much could you expect to find looking through the windows?"

He laughed. "I wasn't looking through the windows."

"You broke in?" She hissed the words as quietly as she could.

"No breaking. Second-story window wasn't locked."

She groaned. "That is so wrong."

"It is and it isn't. Not when the stakes are so high. And she'll never know I was there. Anyway, nothing to tie her to the Collective that I could find."

"Well, that's good. Right?"

"I suppose. But the woman has a lot of debt. And very little saved for retirement. That might be enough to make a person do questionable things."

"How much would the Collective pay for the book?"

"Whatever it took. Seven figures. More. Money

is not an issue for them." He glanced up and stopped talking.

Macy had arrived with their milk shakes in tall glasses. The whipped cream had been topped with a stemmed cherry. "Here you go. Be right back with your food."

"Thanks." Charlotte took a long pull on the straw. The shake was perfect: cold and creamy and deeply chocolatey. "Mmm. That is exactly what I needed right there."

Walker swallowed a mouthful of his shake. "You've had a really hard day."

She let out a long sigh. "I wonder when I'll be able to get back to my place. It's a mess. I really need to get it cleaned up before I can live there again."

Macy returned with their plates, which were heaped with food in typical Chickadee's style. "Anything else I can get you?"

"I think we're good," Charlotte said.

Walker nodded as he picked up his fork. "Yep."

Macy left. Walker dug into the meat loaf. "I'll help you straighten it up. I wasn't kidding about that."

"I know you said that, and it's a kind offer, but..." She buttered the roll that had come with the meal. "Won't you be off on your next assignment?"

"They don't typically come one right after the other. And I'll make the time."

"Well, that's nice of you. Thanks. Where is your home really?"

He told her about the little town he lived in and she spent the rest of the meal finding out who the real Walker Black was. He was pretty much the same guy that she'd thought, just some of the details were different. By the end of the meal, she felt like she knew him well.

And witch hunter or not, she still liked him. A lot. It had been a long time since she'd had such a nice conversation with a guy. Walker was easy to talk to. And easy to look at, which didn't hurt either.

As Macy dropped off the check and some boxes for the food they couldn't finish, Charlotte's phone chimed with an incoming text. She checked it while Walker paid.

It was Lola. *All auras unblemished. Don't know what to tell you. Should I alert the coven about the book since they're all clean?*

Charlotte looked up at him. "Hey, it's Lola. She says no luck with the rest of the local circle, which is good because I'd hate to think one of those nice ladies was involved in this, but it means we still don't know who took the book. And she wants to know if she should tell the coven about the book being missing?"

He shook his head. "No. I don't want it known that the book is even back in town. Not yet."

"Okay, I'll tell her." She sent Lola his answer, then put the phone away.

Walker had already packed up her food. "Ready to go? I'm sure Edgar Allan is ready for you to be home."

"Oh! Edgar Allan! Yes, let's go." No matter how bad her day had been, a little snuggling with her cat would help.

And maybe, if Walker played his cards right, he'd get a little snuggling too.

Chapter Fifteen

Edgar Allan came running toward them as soon as they walked into the apartment. He let out a meow as Charlotte scooped him up. "Hi, baby. How are you? Is it weird being in a strange place?"

Walker raised an eyebrow at the tufts of orange cat hair decorating the last cushion on the beige sofa. That was new. But removable. Somehow. Despite being a feline shifter, cat hair cleanup wasn't something he knew a lot about. And actually, he wasn't sure the Marlboro House even allowed pets, but the landlord would just have to get over it. Walker wasn't about to kick Charlotte and her cat out. It was nice having company around. Well, it was nice having *them* around. There wasn't anyone else he was interested in entertaining. "I'd say he settled in just fine."

Charlotte glanced over. "Oh. Yikes. Sorry about

the fur. I have a lint roller that will clean that up. And I'll brush him so that doesn't happen again. By which I mean it won't happen as much." She shrugged. "Cat hair is an inevitable part of life when you have a cat, especially a long-haired one. With this much fur."

"It doesn't bother me." He smiled. It really didn't. A little errant cat hair was a small price to pay for time with her.

Before she could respond, her phone buzzed. She shifted Edgar Allan over her shoulder like a baby so she could dig it out of her purse and answer it. "Hello? Hi, Millie. Isn't it late for—" Charlotte frowned. "A library emergency?" She rolled her eyes at Walker. "Oh. No, that is important. Yes, I can come. Right now. Fine." She hung up.

Walker wasn't sure he'd heard right. "What kind of a library emergency could there be at nearly ten at night?"

"Apparently, we're having a surprise inspection tomorrow morning. She wants me to meet her there now to get some things done before the inspector arrives. She says he'll be there too early to get every-thing handled."

Walker made a face. "Are surprise library inspections actually a thing?"

"Not really, but this is sort of a special case. She applied for a grant from some charitable organization. I guess we're in the running for the money, which is why the inspector is coming."

"So you're really going to go?"

Her lips pressed together and she exhaled through her nose. "I don't have much choice. She writes my performance evaluations. And she sounded odd. Like she was really nervous. If she's that stressed out about the inspection, I don't want to leave her hanging."

"You want me to come with you?"

"Hah! No. That's sweet of you, but Millie would freak out. More than she already is. Plus Edgar Allan's been alone all day. I brought some of his cat toys in that tote bag. Maybe you could play with him a little? I'll be as quick as I can."

"Okay. I understand. And I'd be happy to play with him."

"Great. He loves the feathers on the fishing pole thing. That will wear him out nicely." She brought the cat closer so she could kiss his furry head. "You like the feather toy, don't you, baby?"

Edgar Allan pawed at a strand of her hair.

She set him down. "Be a good boy."

"I'm sure he will be." Walker leaned in and kissed her cheek. "See you when you get back."

Her cheeks went a little pink, which was incredibly charming. "You don't have to wait up."

"Like hell I don't."

She bit her lip like she was trying to hold back a smile. "Okay, see you when I get back."

She left. Walker found the toy and played with Edgar Allan until he stopped chasing the pretty colored feathers and just lay on the floor waiting for them to come to him. Walker laughed. "Lazy bones."

He put the toy away and went to get himself a beer from the fridge. He drank it looking out one of the dormer windows, watching for the headlights of Charlotte's car. Edgar Allan jumped up to sit on the sill. Walker scratched the cat on the head, and the animal started to purr. It was a comforting sound. Walker wondered what Edgar Allan would do if he purred right back at him. Or shifted into his leopard form.

That might not go as well.

He contented himself with just petting the cat, but by the time the beer was half gone, he still hadn't seen any sign of Charlotte's return. His witch hunter senses began to niggle at him, but he told himself that nothing odd was going on. Charlotte wasn't alarmed by the call, so there was no reason for him to be paranoid about it either.

He hoped.

Another few minutes passed. He ditched the bottle and the last swig of beer, no longer able to ignore the foreboding in his gut. He called Charlotte's cell phone. Straight to voicemail. He found

Millie's cell number in the file that Stillwell had sent, and rang her. Also straight to voicemail. Finally, he pulled up the library's phone number and dialed. It rang six times. The alarm in his head got louder each time. He hung up on the seventh. "I don't like that, Edgar Allan. I don't like it at all."

What kind of library prep could make Charlotte and Millie both too busy to answer the phone?

With the knot in his stomach growing ever tighter, he grabbed his jacket and keys, and ran down the stairs to his truck.

His gut rarely failed him, but this time, he prayed it was wrong.

CHARLOTTE PARKED in the rear of the library like Millie had told her to. There wasn't a place to put her car in with Millie's car already there, so she had to block Millie, but Charlotte figured that was no big deal considering that she'd shown up to work at ten p.m. That was about as above and beyond the call of duty as you could get. Honestly. And if that didn't earn her some parking freedom, then nothing would.

She tried the back door, but it was locked. She knocked, wondering if she should dig her key out or wait for Millie to answer, all while trying to maintain a positive, helpful attitude. The library could definitely use the grant money, but honestly, this had better not take long. Not when she could be snuggling or *something* with Walker. And hello, it was a Friday night. Maybe Millie didn't have a life, but Charlotte did. Sure, her social calendar had only recently filled up, but that was beside the point.

She thought about that a second. It was Friday night. Which meant the inspection was happening on a Saturday. That seemed…odd. Even for this grant situation. What was Millie up to?

She was about to get her key out of her purse when something hard poked her in the side.

"Aren't you the dutiful employee?" a voice snarled.

She turned. And sucked in a breath at the sight of the gun in her ribs. And who was holding it. "What are you doing? Is this some kind of joke?"

"No joke. What does it look like I'm doing?" Judge Turnbury growled. "Move. Back in the car. We'll have to take yours since you blocked the old biddy's in."

Charlotte took a few halting steps toward the vehicle and stopped. Was Judge Turnbury having some kind of dementia episode? He'd been a tough judge, but this was…nothing like she'd ever seen from him before. "I don't understand."

"You don't need to. Time's running out." He poked her with the barrel of the gun again. "Just keep moving."

She started walking, still unable to get her head around the fact that this was sweet old Judge Turnbury in front of her. With a gun. And an attitude. "This isn't you. You're such a nice man. And not usually this…mobile."

He snorted. "And you're gullible. You believed exactly what I wanted you to believe."

Maybe she was gullible, but the judge's old-man act had been pretty convincing.

He gestured toward the car with the gun. "Get in. Try anything funny and you'll regret it."

She already regretted coming here. She opened the door and slid behind the wheel. "Where are we going?"

"My house." He kept the gun trained on her as he walked around the front of her old Explorer and got into the passenger's seat.

"I don't know where you live." It was a stall tactic and a lie, but the only thing she could think of. How was she going to get out of this? Where was Millie? If the judge thought Charlotte was going down without a fight, he was wrong.

"You know where I live, everyone knows where I live. Big white house on Elderberry Lane."

"Oh right." She dropped her keys. On purpose. Maybe if she stalled long enough, Walker would come looking for her. But how long was long enough? An hour? Two? She bent down to fish for them and prayed she could think of something else to buy time. Maybe she could magically give the car a flat tire. Or engine trouble. But she didn't have any idea what kind of spell would do that.

The judge grabbed her by the hair and yanked her upright.

"Ow!"

"Stop playing games. Drop the keys again and I'll break one of your fingers. Or worse. Understand?"

Nothing about him looked like he was kidding. She nodded and started the car. She was a few minutes on the road before she found her voice again. "Are you going to kill me?"

He laughed. "No. Not yet anyway."

"What do you want me for?"

He smiled. She'd never noticed how evil the judge's smile could be. It was more of a sneer, really. She wanted to punch him right in the dentures. "You're going to help me read that book."

"What book?"

"You know what book. Middian's."

With a gasp, she glanced at him. "You stole it? You?"

"Didn't think I was capable, did you?"

"Not even remotely. But it's not just that. For one thing, you're a very respected man in this town. You were a judge, for crying out loud. You're supposed to be all about upholding the law, not breaking it. For another, why would you want a book like that when you can't even use it? And how do you know about it?"

He waggled the gun at her. "There's a key for every lock. And you're the key for that book. I don't need to be able to use it, I just need to make you do it for me."

She noticed he hadn't answered her other question. "What's your end goal, then? What is it you think you can get the book to do for you?"

"None of your business." He sat back a little, but the gun stayed aimed at her.

She tried to ignore that in favor of thinking through his motives. What could he want? But the answer to that eluded her, and her thoughts drifted to Millie. What had the judge done with her? Because that seemed like the obvious explanation as to why she hadn't been at the library.

Unless she *had* been at the library and Charlotte just hadn't seen her. Maybe Millie was inside right now wondering where Charlotte was. Maybe she'd call the sheriff when Charlotte didn't show. Hope sprang to life in Charlotte's soul. Good old, by-the-book Millie. There was no way she'd let Charlotte's failure to show slide by.

Unless she was hurt. She glanced at the gun again. There was no telling what the judge had done to her. And to think Charlotte had lit a love candle for Millie with the judge as the target. Egads.

"Slow down, you're going to miss it. And I'd hate to shoot you over a silly thing like that."

That snapped Charlotte out of her thoughts. She slowed down in time to pull into the judge's driveway.

"Park in the back."

Where the car couldn't be seen. She pulled around. And saw the garage door was up.

"Straight in."

She did as he said, then parked. Her hope of being rescued dimmed. No one would have a clue what had happened to her. "Have you been coming to the library all these years because you were trying to find the book?"

He ignored her question. "Out and into the house."

"Are you working for the Collective?"

A flash of something passed through his gaze, but his only answer was a stern, "Out."

She got out of the car, looking around the garage for something she could use as a weapon while the judge exited on his side. There was lots of yard stuff. A shovel. Hedge trimmers. A hoe. The garage door started going down. Maybe she could levitate the trimmers into her hand. She reached out toward them.

"Don't even think about it," the judge said, shoving the gun into her back again. "Into the house, then into the basement."

"Isn't that kind of a cliché? I mean, the basement's so expected." Apparently fear made her chatty. "The front porch, now that would be—"

"Move." He jabbed her.

She moved. Up the steps, then into the house. His home was beautifully finished with wide moldings and expensive trims, even in the mudroom. But then she supposed judges made good money. So why would he want the book? Or be working for the Collective?

"That door," he indicated.

She opened the polished wood panel door and peered down. It was dark. And the stairs didn't exactly inspire confidence. Or match the fine detail of the rest of the house. "How about a light? Unless you want me to trip and break my neck. Can't really help you if I'm dead, now can I?"

"Switch is on the side of the wall."

She found it and turned the lights on. The cellar had a dirt floor, she could tell that much. And there were cobwebs. Which made her shudder.

"What was that?"

"What was what?"

"That. What you just did. Don't try anything witchy. Won't work on me."

She doubted that. She turned a little to see him. "I shuddered because there are cobwebs down there and I hate spiders. If you have a problem with that, tough. I can't do anything about my involuntary reactions."

"All right, relax." He held his hands up to emphasize his words. Which meant for once, the gun wasn't pointed at her.

She took the opening. She shot her fingers toward him and sent a bolt of magical electricity through him.

It bounced off him and hit her, knocking her into the door and sending her to the floor in a heap. The magic zipped through her, a million hot little wasps stinging relentlessly, then it was gone. She tried to catch her breath. So that's what that felt like.

"I told you not to try anything." He leaned over her. "I'm about to have you use one of the most powerful grimoires on the planet. Did you really think I wouldn't have some kind of protection against magic?"

She swallowed, but her mouth was so dry that her tongue stuck to the roof of her mouth. She peeled it free so she could answer. "Apparently, I did."

Chapter Sixteen

The library was dark, which was exactly what Walker had expected to find but everything he'd hoped against. At least with a light on inside, there might be a chance they were actually in there working. He parked the truck at the curb and ran to the front door to peer in. Dark. Not even lights in the back where the office was.

He smacked his fist on the glass and let out a curse. He stood there for just a second, letting his anger get the best of him, letting the reflection of his glowing eyes stare back at him. But only for a second, because Charlotte needed him.

Then it was time to do what he'd been trained to do. A little witch hunt. Namely for the one responsible for Charlotte's disappearance. He didn't know who that was yet, but he would find her, because there was no way on earth he wasn't going to rescue the one he really cared about.

Tracking wasn't something he did well in this form, though. He needed his leopard form. Instinct made him look around for watching eyes even though he knew he was alone. With that confirmed, he was about to shift when he realized he was letting his emotions get in the way of his thinking. He'd been trained better than that. And Charlotte needed him at his best.

He hadn't done a perimeter check yet. Millie parked behind the library.

He got in his truck and raced around to the back. There was a car parked there. Not Charlotte's old Ford Explorer, but he recognized the car all the same.

It was Millie's Kia sedan. But she wasn't in it and there had been no sign of her in the library. A new alarm went off in his head. Had both women been taken?

He left the truck behind her car and jumped out to inspect the Kia. It was an older vehicle but in great shape. Probably because Millie took care of it so that it would last and she wouldn't be saddled with the expense of a new one. He walked around the car like he had once before, looking inside for any clue that might tell him what had happened. He used the flashlight on his phone to get a better look, but his shifter eyes didn't need much light.

He stared into the car. Something was off. He just wasn't sure what. He stared harder, willing himself to understand what had changed.

It came to him a second later. The seat. Millie was a tall woman. A good head taller than Charlotte, but not quite as tall as he was. The seat was pulled up too close. Her knees would have been pressed into the steering column. No way would she have driven like that.

He was looking for someone short. Someone Charlotte's size. An uncomfortable thought began to form in his mind. A thought he really didn't want to have. Was Charlotte involved in this after all? Where was her car?

He'd never checked her bag to see if the book had actually been stolen. For all he knew, she'd had the book the whole time and had made up the story about it being taken to throw him off.

No, he refused to believe that the Charlotte he knew would do that. It was a dark path he didn't want to go down. Not about her. Not about the woman he'd come to care for.

But she was a witch. And if the FOL had taught him anything, it was that witches were not to be trusted.

A new anger curled up his spine. If Charlotte was involved, if she had lied to him, he'd have no problem turning her over to the FOL.

But he couldn't bring himself to believe that was

possible and the anger died a quick death. Charlotte was the victim here. He was certain of that. He rubbed a hand across his face and the now familiar scent of Edgar Allan filled his nose. He looked at the cuff of his shirt. A few orange strands of fur were stuck to his sleeve.

Cat hair. He stared at it for a second as something new jogged loose in his brain. But what did cat hair have to do with anything? He closed his eyes and thought. Why was cat hair important? There was something about it just at the edge of his memory. Something he needed to remember. Was it about the hair Edgar Allan had left on the sofa? No, that wasn't it.

Think.

Cat hair somewhere else? He opened his eyes. Cat hair *on* someone else. Orange cat hair. Edgar Allan's to be exact.

Walker let out a low curse at the idea forming in his head. He took a deep inhale just to be sure. Liniment. It was faint, but it was in the air.

That confirmed Walker's suspicions.

Judge Turnbury was about a foot shorter than Millie, and he'd been late to the library the morning of the break-in. Charlotte had pointed that out. And when he had arrived, he'd had orange cat hair on his sleeves too. As if he'd picked up a cat and carried it somewhere. Like a bathroom for safe keeping.

Maybe the judge had a long-haired orange cat just like Edgar Allan. Or maybe he'd been in Charlotte's apartment. What were the odds that the feeble old man wasn't so feeble? Hell, he might not even be an old man. Walker's ire went up thinking about how quickly they'd dismissed the judge as a possible suspect.

Walker didn't have time to wait for Stillwell to find out if the man had a cat or where the man lived or what his health was like. Finding Turnbury wasn't as important as finding Charlotte and he could do that on his own. He took a few seconds to send Stillwell a text: *It's happening. It's the judge.*

Stillwell was smart enough to figure that out. Then Walker locked his truck and shifted into his leopard form, his clothing transforming into his animal skin with the magic of his true self. He stood still for the brief moment it took the change to settle over him, letting the crystalline night air ruffle his fur. He loved being in this form. But he could go for a nice long run later.

Right now, he had work to do. He lifted his muzzle into the breeze and inhaled, searching for Charlotte's unique scent and any faint traces of liniment.

He found both pretty quickly. He focused on hers. The warm, sort of lemony smell made him think of summer days. He took off, following that fragrance. There was a third scent in the mix. One he couldn't immediately separate into distinct notes. Millie's maybe. But it was also a little sour, and that part he knew. The smell of dark magic. Whoever that smell belonged to, they'd been doused in it.

Didn't mean that person was part of what was going on. They could also be a victim of dark magic. It could have been used to restrain or immobilize the women.

Either way, it was a sign that he was on the right track.

He put his head down and kept going.

CHARLOTTE WENT down the stairs as slowly as she could, but that earned her a few more pokes with the gun barrel. She was going to have a nasty bruise on her ribs. *If* she lived through this.

She really hoped she would. Who would take care of Edgar Allan if she didn't?

"Hurry up." The judge was not a patient man. She added that to his list of failings, which was getting pretty long.

"Yeah, yeah." That was as snappy a response as she could come up with while faced with the thought of orphaning her sweet fur baby. Would the judge actually shoot her? She tended to think he would. At least she'd gotten to kiss Walker. Maybe she'd focus on that right before the judge pulled the trigger. Then she could die with a smile on her face. Hmm. Maybe Walker would be so despondent with grief that he'd adopt Edgar Allan just to keep her memory alive.

She might be getting a little melodramatic, but how nice would it be for her fur baby to be raised by someone who could actually turn into a cat?

They got to the bottom of the stairs and the judge flipped another light switch. It turned on a single bulb in a grungy porcelain socket in the middle of a low ceiling.

"Millie," Charlotte gasped.

Millie Merriweather was duct-taped to an old wooden chair and seemed to be passed out, based on the slump of her head and body and her general non-responsiveness. There was a second wooden chair beside her, but it had been knocked over. Maybe she'd done that.

Racks built from two by fours and plywood lined the back and side walls. A few dusty canned goods with faded labels sat on the shelves, along with some random cardboard boxes and old coffee cans filled with junk. A rickety toboggan leaned against one of the racks, a couple of ski poles next to it. And there were cobwebs everywhere. Typical New England basement. Except for the unconscious, restrained woman.

Charlotte shook her head in disgust. "You're an awful man, Gilbert." He didn't deserve the title judge. Or the respect that came with it. "What did you do to Millie?"

"Nothing, just knocked her out. She'll be fine." He nudged Charlotte forward. "Go over to the first rack on the right and zip tie one wrist to it. Zip ties are in the Folgers can."

Seeing Millie so helpless like that had really gotten Charlotte's anger up. "And if I refuse?"

He narrowed his eyes. "I'll shoot Millie."

"You wouldn't." But he probably would. Charlotte hated him even more. She walked over and did as he commanded, taking a black zip tie out of the can and putting it around her wrist. She dropped it on the first try without meaning to.

Then she dropped it again on purpose. If he wanted her zip tied, he was going to have to do it himself, which meant getting him close. He might have only been pretending to be frail earlier, but he still wasn't a spring chicken. And while she wasn't trained in any kind of self-defense, she bet a knee to the groin would do wonders. "I can't do this one-handed."

He wiggled the gun at her. "I'm not coming over there. Get it done or we'll see how much Millie bleeds."

"I can't believe you were the icon of justice in this town. Your wife would be so ashamed of you. What would she think about you being in bed with the Collective?"

"Shut up about my wife," he screamed, sending a shower of saliva into the air.

Gross. But good to know she'd found a weak spot. He also hadn't denied working with the Collective. "You know I'm right."

He pointed the gun at her, his chest heaving. "Get those zip ties on *now*."

She frowned. So much for that. It wasn't worth trying to make him stroke out if she got shot in the process. But at least she'd be able to leave the zip tie loose. And maybe the edge of the can was sharp enough to saw through one of these things. If she got the chance to try that, she would. She pushed the pointed end through the connector end. "There."

"Tighter. No gaps."

She glared at him and pulled it tighter. It was a little shocking how much she wanted to shove her knee into the bits and pieces of a senior citizen.

"Good." He tucked the gun into his waistband. "I'll be right back. Don't go anywhere." He laughed like he'd just told the best joke ever and went upstairs.

"Jerk," she muttered after him. At least he'd left the light on. She started searching the shelves around her for something to cut the plastic around her wrist, but there was a reason he'd put her on this side. Other than the Folgers can full of zip ties, and a Maxwell House can with a couple inches of soot

KRISTEN PAINTER

in it, the shelves were empty. Too bad she wasn't some kind of special ops genius who could whip up a bomb out of those ingredients. She should have read more Clancy. Or watched more MacGyver.

She stretched her fingers toward the zip tie can and tried to levitate it closer.

A soft moan penetrated the stillness.

Charlotte glanced over and the can thumped down onto the shelf. Millie seemed like she was waking up. Charlotte was maybe half a foot behind her on the other side of the cellar, so she leaned forward. "Psst. Millie. Are you okay? How are you doing?"

Millie lifted her head and looked around in that groggy, sort of bobble-head kind of way that reminded Charlotte of a newborn baby. Or someone who'd had a little too much to drink. Or, you know, been recently knocked unconscious. "Charlotte?"

"Behind you a little."

Millie turned her head. Her eyes were half-shut. "What are you doing here? Where is here?"

"We're in Judge Turnbury's root cellar. And I'm here because he kidnapped me too."

That didn't seem to help Millie. "We got kidnapped?" She tried to lift her arm. "Is that why I'm tied to this chair? Why did we get kidnapped?"

"Technically, you're duct-taped. And it's because of me. I'm so sorry."

Millie shook her head once, then grimaced like that had been a bad idea. "Why is it your fault?"

Charlotte sighed and leaned against the rack. How had Walker ever thought Millie was involved? "You know that ratty old book that came through the book return slot? The one you threw away? I rescued it from the trash and it turns out, it's pretty valuable. Gilbert wants it. Sort of."

That didn't seem to jive with Millie. "That book was rubbish."

"It wasn't, I swear."

"How could you tell? The pages were glued shut."

"I could tell because…" She really wasn't supposed to reveal that she was a witch to anyone outside the coven, but then, she hadn't taken the oath to join the coven yet. And if she was going to end up dead, what did it matter? It was a lot to process.

Millie tried to sit up a little more. "That book is magic, isn't it?"

Well, that solved that. "Yes. How did you know?"

Millie stared straight ahead and went silent for a moment. "My mother was a witch."

If Charlotte hadn't been attached to the shelves, she probably would have fallen over. "For real?"

Millie nodded slowly. "Yes." She exhaled a long, slow breath. "I had a feeling about that book. That's why I threw it away. I didn't want a grimoire in the library. Didn't want a book like that to fall into the wrong hands. Guess it's too late for that."

Was Millie implying that Charlotte's hands were the wrong ones? Or Judge Turnbury's? "What do you mean it's too late?"

"I…" Millie looked over at her. "Why are we here again?"

"Because the judge stole the book and he wants me to use it for him."

Millie's head lolled to the side. "You're a witch too."

Charlotte took a deep breath. "I am."

"And you can…operate this book?"

"That's what everyone seems to think."

Millie blinked a few times. "He's going to kill us, you know."

"I don't think he'll really—"

"He told me if things didn't go his way, he would make sure all traces of his mistakes were gone. What do you think that means?"

Charlotte swallowed. Sounded like the judge was going to kill them. "I think it means we're in trouble."

Millie's eyes were round and liquid with fear. "Do whatever he wants and get us out of here. Please. I don't want to die."

"I don't either."

"Good," Millie choked out. There was an edge

of hysteria in her voice. "Because if I die and you're to blame, so help me I will come back and haunt you to death myself."

Charlotte just nodded. Now was not the time to remind her boss that they'd probably both be dead. "I'll keep that in mind."

Chapter Seventeen

Walker realized pretty quickly that traveling in leopard form wasn't so easy in a town full of people who were out and about on a Friday night. The Cranberry Festival had swelled the town's population, and most of those visitors had no desire to be inside when there were bands to hear, games to be played, crafts to buy, and heart-attack-inducing foods to be eaten.

The town was also better lit than usual, thanks to the Festival, meaning that many of the shadows that might normally conceal him weren't there. He had no choice but to shift back to his human form until he got through the madness of Main Street and into the residential area.

Here, among the homes, there were enough shadows. He slunk between houses, going around those that were ablaze with lights, to pick up Charlotte's scent again on the other side. Her scent was getting stronger, as was the sour stench of dark magic.

It almost overwhelmed him behind the next house, enough so that he shifted into human form to get a better look. Was he at Judge Turnbury's? He picked his way around the side until he came to a window. The house was dark inside like no one was home. He went as close to the front as he dared.

And picked up another scent he recognized. This was Lola Honeycutt's house. Charlotte's mentor. For a woman who proclaimed none of the witches in town would have anything to do with dark magic, her house reeked of it. That was new. He would never have missed it before.

Maybe because the grimoire hadn't been there before. That could be the sourness filling his nose. But he'd had Middian's in his hands and the smell hadn't been this strong. Could it be the stench increased if the book was used? Or maybe Lola had recently cast some new, dark magic spells.

Either way, Charlotte could be in worse trouble than he'd imagined. He prayed that wasn't the case, but there was no telling what dark magic had been unleashed. Or where Charlotte was. Turnbury might have taken her, but he could be in league with Honeycutt. That would explain why the witch's house stank of dark magic.

In fact, the stench was too powerful to ignore.

The book was here. It had to be. Which meant Charlotte probably was too. They could have taken her to lure him in. Or they could have snatched her to shut her up about the book. Or they might need her because she was the only one who could open the book. If that was the case, they'd have to force her to do the bonding ritual too, or she wouldn't be able to cast any of the spells in the book.

Once she bonded with the book, the FOL would never release her. His heart sank with that terrible realization. They'd lock her and the book away. After he turned them both in. He swallowed against the bitter taste in his mouth.

The thought of her in FOL custody chilled him. Charlotte wasn't a bad witch. She was kind and generous and good. But being locked up in the FOL cells would change all that. It would destroy her.

He couldn't let that happen.

Still in human form, he started around the home's perimeter, listening carefully for signs of life while he looked for a way into the house. All while hoping he wasn't too late.

***

GILBERT'S CLOMPING footsteps announced his return to the basement before Charlotte actually saw him. When he appeared on the lower half of the stairs, all she could focus on was the book tucked under his arm.

Middian's.

What kind of man spent his career working for justice, then turned into a scheming, lying, power-hungry thief? And went to work for a group like the Collective? That low-life piece of trash, that's who. Charlotte had never considered herself a violent woman, but she was rethinking that in a big way.

The judge smiled grimly at Millie. "I see you're awake, Ms. Merriweather."

"Go suck an egg, Gil."

"Tsk, tsk. Such language from the head librar-ian. Maybe I should slap some duct tape over your mouth."

Millie shut up.

Gilbert approached Charlotte, but not too close. He patted the book under his arm. "Time to get to work. I assume you've completed the bonding ritual?"

She hadn't, but lying about it could buy her some time. "Yep."

"Excellent." He put the book on the shelf nearest her and shoved it so that it slid close enough for her to reach it. "Open the book and find the spell for resurrection."

"Um…what?"

"You heard me. Resurrection."

"Who do you think I'm going to resurrect?"

His eyes sparkled with manic intensity. "My wife, of course."

Which was both sweet and creepy and probably how the zombie apocalypse started. "Gilbert, she's been gone for five—"

"Six," he corrected. "Six years."

"Okay, even worse. I don't think you want to see what she looks like right now. Bringing her back to life in her current state would be…really unfortunate."

"I know exactly what she looks like. Her ashes are in that Maxwell House can. The spell will restore her beautifully, you'll see."

Charlotte grimaced. "That's your wife in that can? Why wouldn't you put her in something, I don't know, prettier?"

"Erma never went for fancy." He laughed, but it ended in a weird sob. "Just get that spell working."

"I will. I promise. Just one question first. How could you join up with a group like the Collective?"

"How? Because they promised me my wife back, you dumb girl. Now get to work on that spell."

But she needed to know a little more. "Then what? You turn the book over to them?"

"Yes. Enough." He gestured with the gun. "The spell."

"On it." Charlotte pulled the book closer as she

opened it. The spell on the page in front of her was for the bonding ritual—Lola had said the book would open to that one—but she wasn't about to perform that one. If only Lola were here now. She'd know what to do.

Charlotte turned the pages as slowly as she could, acting like she was studying each one. This was a game she could play indefinitely, but she hoped it didn't take that long for Walker to show up. He had to be looking for her by now, right?

The spells in the book got darker the deeper in she went, the illustrations more twisted. She got the sense they were written in a variety of languages, all magically translated as her gaze fell upon the words.

The eerie knowledge that the book was *aware* of her settled over Charlotte like a damp fog. She couldn't shake the prickliness of it, and couldn't wait to be done with this wretched thing.

She came to the resurrection spell at about one-third in, which said volumes about what the rest of the book held. It creeped her out just to have her hands on it now, knowing what sort of awful things it was capable of. This book should absolutely be locked away. She stared at the spell, wishing she hadn't found it.

"Did you find it?"

She looked up to see the gun still in his hand. She sighed. "Yes, I found it. But I need to read it first and understand it. I imagine you want me to get this right the first time."

"Yes. But if I think you're procrastinating…"

She read the first few lines of the spell. Then read them again before answering him. "You'll what?"

His brows lifted. "I'll put some lead in Millie."

Charlotte pursed her lips as a burst of inspiration came to her. Sometimes, deceit had its uses. "You'd better not. Unless you want Erma to take possession of a holey body."

"What?" Millie strained to look at her. "Are you saying you're going to put his dead wife into my body?"

Charlotte tapped the book with her free hand and did her best to lie convincingly. "That's what it says this spell does. Resurrects the spirit, not the body, then puts it in a new host."

"No," Gilbert snarled. "I want my wife back just like she was, not my wife in Millie's body."

"How do you think I feel?" Millie snapped. "Enough of this. I want out. Now. Cut me loose, Gilbert." She struggled against the duct tape, straining and getting nowhere.

"Sorry," Charlotte said. "That's what this spell does."

Gilbert cursed before speaking to Charlotte. "It's better than nothing, I guess. Do you need Millie conscious for the spell to work?"

"I don't think so, why?"

"Gil," Millie barked. "Cut me loose."

Gilbert walked over and clocked her on the head with the butt of the gun. "You're not going anywhere." She slumped down as he swiveled back toward Charlotte. "Get on with it."

"Right." Crap. Crappity crap crap. Charlotte's pulse kicked up. She stared at Millie, trying to think of some way to stall, but she was running out of ideas.

"Now." He aimed the barrel at her. "Start casting, witch."

"I haven't read it all the way through yet. I need to finish that first." Maybe she shouldn't have lied about this spell. Or about having completed the bonding ritual. Gilbert was really going to be mad when he found that out.

He waved the gun around. "What are you waiting for? Read!"

"Okay, reading." She swallowed and focused her gaze on the book again.

Upstairs, a door closed with a dull thud. She and Gilbert looked up at the same time, but the sound only held Gilbert's attention for a second. He grew frantic. "No more reading. Cast it now. *Now.*"

Charlotte's spirits soared. That had to be Walker. "I'm down here," she shouted. "In the basement."

The cellar door opened, and Charlotte almost

held her breath with joy. But the feet that appeared on the steps were not Walker's.

The kitten-heeled black lace-up boots were only a temporary disappointment. As soon as Charlotte recognized them, she smiled.

Her mentor stopped at the bottom of the landing and took in the scene before her with a stern expression. "Well, well."

"Lola, you're here! And just in time. How perfect!" Charlotte was gushing a little, but if there was ever a time for gushing, it was now. "How did you find me? You know what? I don't care. I'm just happy to be rescued. Thank you! But watch out for the judge. He's got some kind of protection spell against magic on him."

"Yes, I know," Lola said. Her eyes tapered as she took in the judge. "I put it there. Perhaps I shouldn't have."

Charlotte's jaw fell open. "What?"

Lola frowned. "Was he trying to get you to perform the resurrection spell?"

"Yes. Why did you give him magical protection?"

"Was he trying to get you to perform the binding ritual too?"

"No, because I told him I already had."

Her body went tense. "Did you?"

"Not yet."

She relaxed. "Good."

"I still don't understand why you'd give him magical protection."

Lola ignored Charlotte, choosing instead to walk over to the judge and backhand him. "You fool. I told you we'd do your spell after mine was finished."

He cowered in front of her. "But you promised. I'll tell the Collective—"

Lola cut him off with a laugh. "You still think we're turning the book over to the Collective?"

"But I promised them—"

"The only reason you're even a part of this, old man, is to keep that group of fanatics off our backs until we have the power we need."

The judge went silent, but Millie had come to life rather quickly at the sound of Lola's voice. The head librarian lifted her chin triumphantly. What she had to be triumphant about, Charlotte wasn't sure. Maybe the fact that her hair still looked perfect.

Charlotte tried to think, but there was so much happening that confusion clouded her ability to make sense of it all. "What's going on? Just tell me in plain English."

Lola smiled at her mentee. "You and I are about to make witch history."

"We are? How?"

"You're going to perform the binding ritual." Lola's smile widened like the Cheshire cat's. "But we're going to use my blood."

Charlotte had a pretty good idea what that meant based on the sinking feeling in her stomach. "You're not on the side of good, are you?"

Lola snorted. "My sweet little mentee. I'm on the same side I've always been on. Mine."

Chapter Eighteen

A kitchen window had provided Walker with the access he'd needed into Honeycutt's, but it took only a few minutes of searching to tell him no one was in the house or the cellar. And even though the search had only taken a few minutes, he'd wasted time, and that amped up his anger. It almost felt like he'd been set up. Or deliberately waylaid. He didn't think Lola was that clever, but as he stood in her kitchen doing one last scan of the place, his irritation grew.

Time to find Charlotte. He climbed out the same window he'd come in through, shifting into leopard form as he dropped to the ground, and took off again, focusing on Charlotte's sweet scent. It was easy to pick up in the crisp evening air now that he'd compartmentalized the sourness of the dark magic.

No more distractions. He wasn't stopping again until he was sure he'd found her. Even if that meant temporarily leaving the book behind. Besides, in less than an hour, the book would be back at the library, and provided he was the first one there to nab it, everything would be fine.

So long as Charlotte's expiration date didn't come sooner. And so long as the book didn't return to her. Which was why he had to find her immediately.

The chilly night air whistled past as he loped through the hibernating gardens of Everlasting's backyards. Leaves and dead grass crunched under his paws. He startled a few housecats out on their nightly wilds, and nearly gave one elderly woman a heart attack while she was walking her dog.

Couldn't be helped. But his instincts told him that any reported leopard sightings in this town would get less attention than they might elsewhere. Especially because he'd crossed the scent path of another shifter, this one wolf.

Everlasting's supernatural population must be bigger than he'd originally suspected.

He ran on, going as fast as he could while holding on to Charlotte's scent. The houses around him were becoming grander. The yards bigger. The neighborhoods quieter. But the bitterness of the dark magic, the thing he'd been tuning out to keep her scent at the forefront, was once again becoming harder and harder to ignore.

It was a good sign *and* a bad one. If there was that much dark magic present where Charlotte was being held, experience told him that this evening's outcome was not going to be pretty. He was prepared for that. Always was on an FOL mission. But this was the first time someone he cared about was stuck in the middle of it.

That changed things. And it would color his decision making. Maybe even his reaction times. It made him feel off-kilter in a way he didn't like at all. The last time he'd been so unsure, he'd been a newly appointed agent on his first mission.

He'd managed that one without things getting too ugly. But again, there'd been no one in the mix to protect, just an object to obtain.

Before he could worry about it a second longer, the lemony-summery perfume he'd come to recognize as uniquely Charlotte hit him hard. He stopped.

He was here. Outside a big manor house that looked like old money. The stench of dark magic wafted through the air with the same power as rotting fish on an August afternoon. There was also the much heavier tang of liniment and one other faint smell. The one that had unlocked this whole thing for him. The faintest whiff of cat, specifically Edgar Allan.

This was the place. Charlotte was here. The book, too.

Walker returned to his human form and flattened himself against the side of the house. He needed to do some recon, figure out where Charlotte was and how many foes he was up against. That would give him the biggest advantage going in.

Then it was time to light this candle.

* * *

CHARLOTTE COULDN'T BELIEVE IT. Her mentor, the woman she looked up to, was not at all who Charlotte had thought she was. She felt deceived. And very, very angry. "You're out for yourself. After everything you told me about the coven being family and how the sacred circle was a sisterhood. Lies. All of it lies."

Lola's eyes narrowed and all traces of amusement vanished. "I did what I had to. Middian's should have been mine. If you hadn't interfered…" She shook her head like she'd been about to say too much.

But Charlotte was too rocked by the betrayal to think about much else. "I'm done. I won't do the bonding spell. I won't help you."

Lola stretched out her hand toward Millie. The

air shivered with magic, moving like a heat wave in the summer, and suddenly Millie jerked against the duct tape, crying out in pain as she went taut with whatever power Lola was using against her.

"Stop," Charlotte cried out.

Lola dropped her hand and Millie relaxed, moaning softly. Lola looked at Charlotte. "You'll do it. Or Ms. Merriweather will pay the price. Is that what you want?"

It really wasn't.

"Please," Millie whispered. "Do what they want. Save me. Please. It's just a book. Who cares?"

Except it wasn't just a book. It was a dangerous tool. And filled with the kind of power that could destroy. But Millie didn't deserve to suffer. Or possibly lose her life. Charlotte could not stand by and watch someone die because of a decision she'd made. Her belly went cold with helpless resignation. "I'll help you. But leave Millie alone."

"Done." Lola snapped her fingers. "Turnbury, the book."

He scampered over and handed her the copy of Middian's, cowering slightly. She put the book on the shelf in front of Charlotte. "Open it to the binding ritual, then start reading."

Reluctantly, Charlotte opened the book, deliberately picking a spot near the back to see if she could stall. "I don't know where the—"

The pages started turning on their own. They stopped after a few moments and the paper floated down to lie flat.

Lola smiled. "The book knows what needs to happen. Now read."

Stupid book. Charlotte huffed out a breath and read through the words as fast as she could to get them over with. "With my blood, I make my solemn promise. With my blood, I bind these precious pages. With my blood, I accept this powerful gift." She looked at Lola. "There, happy?"

From the belt at her waist, Lola unsheathed her ceremonial dagger and held the point of the athame up. She pricked her finger on it and squeezed until a drop of blood appeared. "Read it again. Slower. Phrase by phrase."

Charlotte frowned. Millie nodded at her, her gaze full of pleading. Charlotte sighed. "With my blood, I make my solemn promise."

Lola tipped her finger so that a drop of blood hit the page. The blood was absorbed instantly. "Keep going."

"With my blood, I bind these precious pages."

The second drop disappeared just as quickly.

"And now the last phrase," Lola commanded.

Charlotte forced herself to finish. "With my blood, I accept this powerful gift."

The third drop touched the page and a spark of magic burned over the book, covering the book in bewitched fire for a second, then vanishing to leave the grimoire transformed. Every last tattered section was restored. The leather turned a rich, supple brown. The fragile, yellowing paper thickened and became creamy, pristine sheets with distinct black ink instead of the faded gray that had been there. Every bit of gold gleamed.

"Perfect," Lola breathed.

"I told you it would work," Millie said. She stood up from the chair as if she'd never been restrained to it.

"You were right," Lola said.

Charlotte stared at the head librarian, once again knocked back by a sharp sense of disbelief. "You're in on this? How did you do that?"

Millie's mouth thinned to her usual disapproving expression. "Do you really not know?" She waved her hand through the air. A trail of brilliantly colored sparks followed behind it. "Magic."

Charlotte shook her head. "How did I not know you're a witch?"

"She was hiding that part of herself." Lola snorted. "An easy enough feat for a witch as powerful as she is. In fact, she's the most powerful one in this town. She's also my mentor and my—"

"You're a witch too? And a dark one." Charlotte's lip curled in disgust. "How long have you been planning all this?" Not once had Charlotte ever suspected her boss had an inkling of magical ability. "I've never seen you at any of the meetings. You never seemed the least bit magical at work." Charlotte had thought by now she could sense other witches. Clearly, she'd been wrong. "But you using magic to hide your magic?"

"Look at you, figuring things out." Millie offered her a patronizing smile. "Now, I understand you have questions, but there's work to be done and I'm not going to interrupt what's begun. You can learn as we go. On to business." Millie pointed a finger at Gilbert and muttered a few words in Latin.

With a loud squeak, he shriveled down to a mouse and ran off into a hole in the wall, his little rodent tail quivering.

Charlotte sucked in a breath. "How did you do that? I tried to zap him earlier and the spell bounced right off him."

Millie smoothed a hand over her hair, which still hadn't budged. "Lola designed the spell so that my magic would still work on him. That's how we do things, Charlotte. You'll see."

No, she wouldn't. Not if it resulted in such awful things. Granted, the judge had sort of deserved that. A little. Except he hadn't actually hurt Millie. Or had he? Charlotte was getting more confused. And starting to freak out. She really didn't want to be a rodent of any kind.

That would not go over well with Edgar Allan. Oh. That was an awful thought. To be eaten by her own cat. She figured it was better to know what lay ahead, so she faced Millie. "Are you going to do that to me too?"

Millie shook her head, lips pursed in her usual dour face. "You're too valuable. We're going to give you the opportunity to join us."

"To join you in what?"

Lola inched forward. "In taking over, that's what. For starters, we're going to turn Everlasting into a haven for witches, then we're moving on to the rest of the state. Then the country." Her voice deepened, edged with ambition. "Then the world."

"All in good time," Millie snapped before addressing Charlotte. "What Lola said is essentially true. We're going to take witches public. No more hiding what we are. It's time witches got the respect they deserve. The book will give us the kind of power that demands that respect."

She spread her hand like she was clearing the way for her words. "I envision a world where we rule like empresses. Any ordinary who tries to stop us will be punished. We will control everything. Magic will become the new currency. And thanks to Middian's, every spell we need to accomplish this is at our fingertips."

Millie was freaking nuts. But Charlotte felt like keeping her talking was also keeping her from using the book, so she asked more questions. "Why give control of Middian's to Lola then? Why not take it for yourself?" That really didn't make sense.

Millie cracked a rare, genuine smile. It was a small one, but a smile nonetheless. "I have as much control over it as she does. The book will read my touch as if it is hers."

Charlotte found that hard to believe. "How is that possible?"

Millie went to stand beside Charlotte's former mentor. "Lola is my daughter."

The ability to speak left Charlotte for a moment. But now that Millie had said it, Charlotte could sort of see the family resemblance. They both had the height. And if Millie put some makeup on, dyed her hair and released it from its hairspray prison, lost the glasses…wow. An older Lola. Scary.

"Didn't see that coming, did you?" Lola said.

"I didn't. At all." Charlotte thought about how the judge had said she was gullible. Apparently he'd been right. It saddened her. And made her realize she had a lot to learn. "I still don't understand how I didn't know Millie was a witch. What kind of magic covers up magic?"

Millie shrugged. "Simple diffusion spell with a more complex blinding spell on top of that."

Charlotte couldn't have done either of those if she'd tried. "And you pretended to be the judge's victim because…?"

Millie's eyes took on a self-satisfied glimmer.

"Because you're too much of a Goody-Two-shoes. You had to be standing right there when I found the book. Had to take it out of the trash before I could retrieve it." She hmphed. "I should have found a reason to stash it in my office. Be that as it may, when the book didn't return itself to the library, we knew it had chosen you. We had to come up with a good reason to make you do what we told you to. We didn't think you'd give the book up any other way."

"You're right," Charlotte said. "I wouldn't have."

Lola tucked her athame back into its sheath on her belt. "Well, kiddo, don't feel bad. Now you can join us and finally get somewhere in life."

The comment created a new surge of anger in Charlotte. "My life is getting somewhere already. Maybe not as fast as I'd like, but I'm doing it honestly."

Lola rolled her eyes. "Oh, brother." She looked at Millie. "I knew she wouldn't come to our side."

"You're right." Charlotte was so mad she wanted to hex them both into oblivion. If she knew how. "I will never join you. Never. So if you're going to kill me or turn me into a mouse or whatever, just do it already, because nothing you say is ever going to sway me to use my gifts for evil."

"She had her chance." Millie hmphed. "Now we have to eradicate her."

"Get it over with, then," Lola said. "I want to use the book already. I get a wish, you know."

"I know." Millie eyed her sternly. "And you already promised to use it to fill our bank accounts."

Lola sighed loudly. "I am."

"Good. Now let me wrap this up." Millie raised her hands to cast the killing spell (or possibly another mousing spell, although based on the word eradicate, things felt more fatal this time), but a loud crash upstairs interrupted her.

A second later, the cellar door came flying down the steps. It hit the wall and splintered as a huge leopard bounded after it. The beast snarled at them, its lips curling back to show teeth the size of the dagger on Lola's hip.

The two witches screeched and retreated behind Charlotte, using her as a shield. Lola whimpered, making Charlotte like her even less. If you were going to act like an all-powerful badass witch, the sudden sight of a giant leopard shouldn't turn you into a sniveling, spineless mess.

Charlotte said a little prayer that this would turn out to be Walker and not some other random leopard. In this town, you just never knew, but there *was* something familiar about the leopard's gaze. *Please let it be him.* Although, if it wasn't and she was about to die, she didn't want to see it coming. She wanted to remember that kiss. She closed her eyes and braced for whatever happened next, all while imagining Walker's mouth on hers.

Another loud snarl ripped through the room, then the softest fur brushed past Charlotte's cheek with a whoosh of air.

Two shrieks filled her ears. She opened her eyes.

Chapter Nineteen

Walker barely contained his rage as he stood over top of the women, growling his heart out. Millie fainted immediately. Kind of surprising for a witch who should have been used to the odd and unusual, but he'd seen stranger things. Lola seemed to be unconscious from hitting her head on the dirt floor. He shifted back into his human form and turned to Charlotte. "You okay?"

"Much better now. I'm so glad it's you." She leaned against the wooden racks.

He laughed. "Do you know another leopard shifter?"

"Actually, I've heard the guy who runs the—" Her eyes went wide. "Lola!"

Walker dodged as a thin blade whipped past his face. He grabbed Lola's wrist and bent it up behind her back, taking the blade away from her and tucking it into his own belt.

She let out a rasp of pain. "You're hurting me."

"Be glad that's all I'm doing to you." He shoved her into the racks and held her there easily. "Still feeling that bite of energy? Or would you rather I shift and let you feel a different kind of bite?"

"Get off me, witch hunter."

"Here." Charlotte held out a handful of zip ties.

He reached out to grab them. "Just what I needed."

He bound Lola's wrists, then attached her to the racks like Charlotte was. He used his thumb to draw the Mobius strip on her forehead while he uttered the FOL's binding incantation. "*Magicae non tenetur omnia.*"

She jerked against the restraint. "What are you doing?"

"Binding your magic. You can still cast spells, but they'll only affect you, so proceed with caution."

"I don't believe you."

He stepped back, smiling. "This should be fun."

She raised her hand and threw a bolt of lightning at him. It never left her fingers. Instead, it traveled back over her hand and sizzled across her body. She twitched and moaned until it died out, leaving her limp and subdued.

"Ouch," Charlotte said.

Walker shook his head. "I warned her."

While Lola muttered angrily at him, he repeated the binding process on Millie. Then he pulled Lola's knife from his belt and twirled it through his fingers while he walked back to Charlotte. "Let's get you free."

"Thanks."

He sliced through the plastic then tucked the knife away. "You sure you're okay?"

She nodded as she rubbed her wrist. "Shaken up. But okay. They turned the judge into a mouse. Not sure we'll ever see him again."

He turned her hands over to look at her wrists himself. "That's one way to tie up a loose end. Or we could bring Edgar Allan in on the job."

"I don't think I want him eating people."

Walker snorted. "No, probably not a good precedent to set."

"By the way, I think the judge was the only one working with the Collective. Apparently, they promised him he could use a spell from the book to raise his wife from the dead."

"I take it that didn't work?"

"Nope. Didn't get as far as trying it really. Millie and Lola interrupted all that. They knew he was working for the Collective, too, but I get the sense they were going along with everything to keep the Collective from guessing their true intent, which was to keep the book for themselves."

"The Collective isn't going to like being double-crossed, but Millie and Lola will be safe in the FOL cells." He laughed. "Really, they should be thanking the FOL for protecting them."

"I doubt that's going to happen."

"Me, either." He leaned in and kissed her, ignored the disgusted grunt Lola made in comment, then pressed his forehead to hers. "I'm so glad you're okay. I wasn't sure I'd get here in time."

"And I'm so glad you figured out where I was."

He leaned back and tapped a finger to the side of his nose. "I'm a pretty good tracker." He pulled his phone out. "I have to call my boss to come take possession of them and the book. One quick question first. Did they force you to bond to the grimoire so that you could use the spells?"

"Not exactly." Charlotte explained what Lola had done with her own blood.

"Hmm. Since it wasn't your blood, I don't know if that means you're bonded or not. You did speak the words. This is a gray area for me." But he knew what Stillwell would think. That Charlotte should be taken into custody just like the other two witches. Walker could not allow that, but he also had to get things tied up here. He dialed Stillwell, resolved to be as vague as possible. The conversation about Charlotte could wait until Stillwell was here in person. And Charlotte wasn't.

Walker's boss answered on the second ring. "Stillwell."

As if Walker didn't know who he was calling. He also knew Stillwell wouldn't be far away. Most likely he was on an FOL plane already landing on a nearby airstrip. "It's done. I'll have the book in safe keeping at my apartment within the next half hour."

"That's all the time you've got. Unless the witch bonded with it."

"I'll find out." Walker checked the time. Twenty-eight minutes until midnight. "Either way, I have it handled."

"Where is the witch?"

"With me. And there's two of them." Stillwell would assume one of them was Charlotte, and Walker was going to let him. He covered the mouthpiece with his hand and looked at her. "What's the address here?"

"19 Elderberry Lane."

He repeated it for Stillwell. "They're in the root cellar, zip tied to the shelving. Their magic is bound. Once I contain the book, I'll bring it back here and meet you to turn it over and give my report."

"You didn't take the case with you?"

"No. I was tracking them. No way to carry it." Stillwell would understand that. It happened often. "When do you think you'll be here?"

"ETA is twenty minutes."

Just like Walker thought, Stillwell was close. "Sounds good. See you then."

Stillwell hung up.

Walker tucked his phone away and checked on Millie and Lola. Millie was just waking up to discover she was zip tied to the rack next to Lola. "You two behave now." He jerked his thumb at Millie but looked at Lola. "Might want to let her know about the boomerang effect. Just in case she decides to try something."

Then he grabbed the book and Charlotte's hand. "Come on, we need to get back to my apartment and lock this thing up. My truck is at the library, but maybe we can find the keys to the judge's car."

"No need. My car is in his garage and my keys are still in it."

He grinned. "Pretty *and* handy. You just get better and better."

CHARLOTTE WENT straight to the couch and hugged Edgar Allan as soon as they got back to Walker's apartment. It suddenly hit her, sitting there, that she'd been about to die. There were no tears, however, just a few deep breaths. And a whole lot of anger.

Walker sat next to her. "I have to return to the judge's house to meet my boss, but I'll be back as soon as I can."

She rested her chin on the top of Edgar Allan's

head. He was purring hard and kneading his paws on her leg. "They were going to kill me because I refused to join them."

Walker brushed a piece of hair off her cheek. "But they didn't. You're safe now. I promise."

She nodded, but the chilling thought hadn't quite let go of her.

"You going to be okay here by yourself? I could call someone to sit with you until I get back."

She offered him a weak smile. "No, I'll be fine. I've got Edgar Allan to keep me company. Just shaken up a little, you know?"

"I do know. I promise I'll be quick. And I'm only a phone call away."

"Good. Thanks."

He stood, the book still in his hands. "If you're asleep by the time I get back, I won't wake you."

"I don't think sleep is very likely."

"I understand that." He took off for his bedroom, returning a few minutes later with a metal box that looked like a steampunk briefcase. The Mobius symbol decorated the tarnished metal. "Okay, I'm out."

She nodded at the case. "Is the book really secure in that thing?"

"It's steel lined with a thin layer of lead, then thin sheets of rock salt, and the whole thing has been enchanted with the same magic I used on

Millie and Lola. It's about as magic-proof as it can be."

"Good." And interesting. "They're mother and daughter, by the way. I had no idea."

"Seems they were keeping all kinds of secrets."

"Apparently." Edgar Allan curled up on her lap and settled in to sleep. "When you get back, I'll tell you everything that happened."

"I can't wait to hear it all." He dangled her keys from his fingers. "Thanks again for letting me use your car."

"Sure. We'll get yours in the morning."

"See you when I get back."

"Bye." She eased Edgar Allan off of her lap and onto the couch, then went to the bedroom to change into her flannel pajamas, which were not the least bit sexy but were very comfortable (and that was all that mattered). She came back to the couch and sat there for a while, just trying to process everything. It was hard. Overwhelming, really. So many things were up in the air now. Would she get the head librarian job? It was a crazy way to get promoted. If it happened.

And what would happen to the coven with Lola gone? Maybe Mena Peabody would take over. If Mena was a good witch. Had any of the other witches in the coven known about Millie and Lola's plan? Would Charlotte get a new mentor? Did she even still want to be a witch? Could you not be a witch if you were a witch?

It was all a muddle of possibilities.

New questions came up about Millie and Lola, too. What exactly was going to happen to them? Charlotte knew they'd be in the custody of the Fraternal Order of Light. But what did that mean? The FOL wasn't exactly a well-known organization. Or was it?

She sighed and looked at Edgar Allan, who was now upside down and snoozing. "You have the life. No job, no bills, no problems. Just love and pets and noms."

She looked toward the kitchen. "Speaking of noms…" She got up to see if there was anything good for a snack. The fact that she had any appetite at all must mean she wasn't as traumatized as she'd thought. Or maybe trauma made her hungry. Hard to say. She'd never had a near-death experience before.

She opened a few cabinets and found a box of protein bars, a vat of peanut butter, an industrial-size sack of beef jerky, a stack of pull-top tuna cans, a bag of coffee, and a loaf of bread. "He eats like a survivalist."

She moved on to the fridge. It held a couple of beers, what looked like a gallon of strawberry jam, a carton of eggs, a stick of butter, and a jar of pickles. She shook her head. "Who lives like this?"

With such slim pickings, she reluctantly made herself a peanut butter and strawberry jam sandwich and took it back to the couch. She put the television on for a distraction and clicked through until she found the first Ghostbusters movie. Seemed oddly appropriate.

The sandwich was surprisingly good. It had been ages since she'd had a PB&J. It was comforting in a way. Like a childhood friend. And with Edgar Allan snuggled up next to her and her soft, flannel jammies on, she could almost forget what she'd been through.

A knock at the door made her put the last half of the sandwich down. She wasn't sure who it would be at this hour. It was after midnight. Could Walker have forgotten his apartment keys? She didn't see them laying around anywhere.

She got up and answered the door. "Did you forget your—oh, you're not Walker."

The thin man's expression remained steely. "No. I'm Stillwell."

"Um, okay, Mr. Stillwell." She had no idea who this guy was, but judging by his suit and tie, he was someone important. Was this Walker's boss? "Can I help you? If you're looking for Walker, he's not here."

"You're Charlotte Fenchurch. You're the witch."

"I don't know if I'm *the* witch." She straightened. "How do you know—"

"You're supposed to be in custody."

"Okay, nope, I'm definitely not that witch." She started to close the door.

He shoved it open.

"Whoa now." She backed up, but Stillwell grabbed her arm. Panic raced through her. "Let go of me."

He pulled out a set of cuffs and was about to slap them on her when her instincts kicked in. She zapped him with a bolt of witchy energy. He jerked back and hit the wall, falling to the floor.

She took off as he climbed to his feet. She scooped Edgar Allan up and kept going to the bedroom. She hip-checked the door shut, dropped Edgar Allan on the bed, and twisted the lock to secure the door. Good thing she'd come in here earlier to change, because she'd brought her purse in when she had. That meant her cell phone was here.

She grabbed it and dialed Walker.

Stillwell pounded on the door. "Open up, witch."

She ignored him to listen to the phone ringing. "Pick up, Walker, pick up." Suddenly her phone started buzzing with an incoming call. She looked at the screen and tapped the button to take the call. "Walker—"

"Don't answer the door."

"Too late. Stillwell is here."

Walker cursed softly. "I'm on my way. I just got a text from him saying he'd meet me at my apartment instead of the judge's so he could take possession of the book immediately. The FOL must be eager to get this thing out of town. Did you let him in? Does he know who you are?"

"I wouldn't say I *let* him in so much as he forced his way in. And does he know I'm Charlotte and that I'm a witch? Yes."

Walker cursed again. And not quite as softly. "Where are you?"

"In the guest bedroom with the door locked. He said I was supposed to be in custody. He tried to put handcuffs on me."

"Tried?"

"I sort of zapped him. Magically."

Walker snorted. "Nicely done. I'm in the parking lot now. I'll get this sorted out as soon as I get up there."

"Okay, good."

Stillwell wiggled the doorknob. "Let me in, witch. The more you fight it, the harder the take down will be."

She didn't even want to think about what that meant. She shouted, "Hurry up," into the phone, then tossed it on top of the dresser and grabbed the chair beside it to wedge under the door handle. "I'm not the witch you want, Mr. Stillwell."

He jiggled the door handle again.

"Seriously, I'm not." Too bad she was just a fledging witch and not a Jedi. If only. She'd use the Force to change his mind. She whispered a protection spell. "The witches you want are the two at Judge Turnbury's house. Walker is on his way to explain everything."

Right on cue, she heard Walker bellow, "Stillwell. Leave her alone."

She put her ear to the door to hear Stillwell's answer.

"You were told to bring her in."

Well now. That was new information.

"I know what I was told. She's not the witch you want."

Charlotte nodded and yelled through the door, "That's what I said."

Stillwell's answer came from farther away, which made her feel a little better. "The book chose her. We need the witch who bonded with the book."

"That's not her. Probably."

Stillwell grunted. "Prove it."

Walker made a sound. A sigh maybe. Then he called for her. "Charlotte, come out here please."

She moved the chair, unlocked the door, then cautiously snuck down the hall and looked out. The two men were in the small living room, faced off. She looked at Walker.

A muscle in his jaw twitched as he made eye contact. The metal case was clutched firmly in his hand. He motioned with a nod of his head for her to join him.

She went to his side, not at all confident that Stillwell wouldn't try to grab her again, but very certain Walker would intervene if he did. "What do you need me to do?"

Walker put the case on the sofa and opened it up, revealing the book. The title's gold letters gleamed at her. She almost reached out to touch it, but curled her fingers into a fist instead.

Walker stood back. "I need you to cast a spell from the book."

Chapter Twenty

"No." Stillwell's response was pretty much exactly what Walker had expected.

He held up his hand. "Hear me out. She can attempt to cast the spell at me. You won't be affected."

Stillwell looked unconvinced. "You would trust a witch?"

"This one? Yes." He glanced at Charlotte. He'd never met a woman like her. He couldn't imagine *not* meeting her. "With my life."

"Then you're a fool because that's precisely what you'll be doing. Trusting her with your life." Stillwell shook his head. "I can't allow it. She could unleash destruction on us. Or the world."

Walker fought hard not to roll his eyes at his boss. He had to remember that Stillwell didn't know Charlotte like he did. "Except that she won't. Not only is she a kind, caring person, but she's not bonded to the book. She won't be able to cast the spell at all."

He sighed. "I'm asking you to trust me. After my years of service, can't you give me that much?"

Stillwell stared at him for a moment. "It's a big risk. One you seem awfully confident about taking. And one that could have extensive consequences. I'm not entirely sure you're not already under one of her spells. This could all be part of her plan."

Walker barely restrained a second eye roll. "It's not. She's been helping me. And she's been the victim here more than anyone else."

Charlotte grabbed the sleeve of his jacket. "Walker, I don't think this is a good idea. What if I *am* bonded to the grimoire?" Her eyes held a sadness he hadn't anticipated. "If I hurt you, I couldn't live with myself. I can't do this."

He took her hand. "You have to. There's no other way to save yourself."

She looked at Stillwell. "There has to be another way. Don't you have a magic test or something you can conduct?"

"No. But I'd be happy to accommodate you if you're thinking about turning yourself in."

She frowned. "No. And you're so helpful." She went back to Walker. "I really don't want to do this."

He squeezed her hand. "You have to, Charlotte.

It's the only way you're not going into FOL custody." At least the only way that wouldn't involve violence, but he didn't want Stillwell to know that he was ready to fight to keep Charlotte free. At least not yet.

She swallowed.

"Fine. Let her attempt it." Stillwell crossed his arms.

"Please, Charlotte," Walker begged. "Do this for me." Because if she didn't, there would be hell to pay. There was no way Stillwell would let her walk without proof of her innocence. And the thought of sweet Charlotte spending the rest of her life locked away in an FOL cell was unacceptable.

She looked like she was on the verge of tears. "You saved my life. Now you're asking me to potentially take yours." She shook her head. "How do I say yes to that?"

"You just do. For me." He lowered his voice. "For *us*."

A single tear rolled down her cheek, but she scrubbed it away with the back of her hand and lifted her chin defiantly. She let out a long sigh, then nodded. "Okay."

She turned her attention to Stillwell. "So you know, I'm barely a witch. I'm a novice. My spell-casting ability is probably equal to yours right now, unless you happen to have some secret magical powers I don't know about. Which is infinitely possible, based on what I've learned recently about my skill in detecting magic in others."

Stillwell snorted.

She continued. "The idea that you think I'm some big, bad, all-powerful witch is laughable. If I was, would I be living in a one-bedroom apartment in the low-rent district? Would I be driving a ten-year-old car? And do you really think that little zap I gave you would have been my best shot?"

Stillwell grunted.

She shook her head. "Walker has told me about the FOL, and it sounds like an organization that needs to exist, especially after what I've seen tonight, but you're wrong about me. One hundred percent wrong."

The hard set of Stillwell's mouth didn't change. "Cast the spell. I'm done waiting."

So was Walker. He wanted this over. He wanted Stillwell gone. And he wanted Charlotte in his arms.

He'd never had doubts about his future with the FOL. Until he'd met her. And now a future with Charlotte was all he could think about.

He just hoped it was still possible after what she was about to attempt.

CHARLOTTE LIFTED the book from the case and opened it. The grimoire warmed in her hands like it had before, coming to life with the same magical energy she'd felt previously. She gave it a moment, to see if it would automatically turn to the binding ritual. It didn't. So was she bonded to it? That uncertain response did nothing to slow her pounding heart or calm her nerves. She would die if she hurt Walker. She owed him her life.

And even though it was probably the dumbest thing her heart had ever done, she was falling for him. The witch and the witch hunter. So help her, when she made bad decisions, she really went big.

She turned the pages, skimming the spells for something as harmless as possible. Hard to do when the book was filled with things like a hex that set the skin on fire, a curse that gave the victim boils on their tongue whenever they spoke, another spell that caused metal to become molten liquid, and a ritual that gave the performer's touch the ability to change raindrops into shards of glass.

When would that *ever* be useful?

None of these were anything she wanted to try. How had she thought keeping this book was a good idea? Of course, that was before she'd looked through it.

Another spell offered transmogrification from human to lizard. Charlotte thought Millie probably knew that one already. Turning the page revealed a spell to turn time back by a day. She thought about that one for a moment until she read on and realized it would only work with a blood sacrifice.

Um, *gross*.

Yet another spell promised to turn the air into acid. She shuddered at the illustration of the spell in action.

"Now, Ms. Fenchurch," Stillwell said.

She looked up at him. "Would you like to pick a spell from this book? Because I have yet to find one I'm willing to risk. Maybe Walker doesn't mean anything to you. Maybe you don't care if I accidentally cause him to be swallowed up in a pit of quicksand, or if he suddenly grows a tail—"

"So, a second tail?" Walker shrugged. "I could deal with that."

She made a face at him. "This isn't easy."

He came closer so he could lean over her shoulder. He pointed at the page she'd just turned to. "What's this one?"

She knew he couldn't see the words. She gave it a quick read. "It renders the subject mute for..." She read further. "Looks like until the subject bends to the wishes of the spell caster."

He nodded. "I can handle that. There. Spell chosen. Cast away."

Stillwell's eyes narrowed. "Don't think you can fake it, either. I can sense magic being used."

She sighed. "Got it. Real magic. Just let me read it through one time." She also had to figure out what she would require of him. Had to be easy in case she was actually able to cast the spell. She glanced up. "Okay. I'm ready."

He took a few steps back. Stillwell did too.

She stretched out her hand and read the spell. "Your voice be silent, your tongue be still! But grant my wish and all be nil. My wish is for a chocolate milk shake from Chickadee's." That was easy enough to make happen.

There was no burst of magical sparks from her fingertips. No weird smoke that floated around Walker. Nothing to indicate the spell had worked, but sometimes magic happened like that.

"Well? Can you talk?"

"I don't know—okay, I do know. Didn't work." Walker grinned and looked at his boss. "There you go. She can't use the book."

Stillwell shook his head as he walked toward Charlotte. "But she just proved she can open the book and read the spells. It's too much of a risk. The witch comes with me."

Chapter Twenty-One

Walker stepped in front of Charlotte. "No, she doesn't. She's not going anywhere. The FOL doesn't need her. *You* don't need her."

Stillwell's eyes narrowed. "Black, you're over-stepping."

Walker didn't move. "You can have the book. You can have the other two witches at the judge's house, but Charlotte goes nowhere. This isn't open for debate."

"Your mission was—"

"To get the book and the witches involved in using it for evil purposes." Walker could feel the big cat coming awake in him. Rising. Stretching. Preparing. "I did that."

Stillwell wasn't backing down. "She can *open* the book."

"So what? She won't have the book. It'll be deep

in the bowels of whatever FOL vault you secure it in."

"Too much of a risk."

"I disagree." Walker shifted into his in-between form, letting his eyes take on the full beast within. Claws sprouted from his fingertips and his voice dropped to a husky growl. His eyes would be glowing, too. Not that any of that would frighten Stillwell. "And I suggest you leave now. Before this goes further."

"Enough," Charlotte said.

But Walker couldn't let this go. And he knew Stillwell wouldn't.

Stillwell's eyes took on the slitted pupils of his own inner beast, and his words rounded with the menacing hiss of his kind. "Are you threatening me?"

"I'm stating facts. And telling you I will defend her."

"This is a line that cannot be uncrossed." Tiny scales appeared over Stillwell's cheeks and across the backs of his hands. He was preparing for a full shift into his cobra form. Preparing to attack.

Just like Walker was. "If taking in an innocent is what the FOL requires of me, then I am no longer interested in being part of the FOL."

Behind him, Charlotte snorted. "Oh, for Pete's sake. I think I know how to solve this once and for all."

He turned just as Stillwell's attention shifted to her too.

She held the book out and whispered a single word in Latin. "*Ustulo*."

The book went up in a burst of white hot flame and vanished in a puff of ashes. They drifted to the floor like dirty snowflakes.

"Finally, that was good for something," she muttered. She brushed her hands off before planting them on her hips. "There. Done. Nothing left to talk about." She pointed at Stillwell. "You, get out. I'm clearly not going with you and I've had a long day and I want to go to bed. Someone has to open the library in the morning."

Then she turned to Walker. "You make sure he leaves."

Walker's inner beast lay down. He nodded. "Will do." Then he turned to Stillwell. "You heard the lady."

Stillwell shook his head. "You're done at the FOL."

Walker watched Charlotte trundle off to bed. As she disappeared from view, he looked at his boss and smiled. "I'm good with that."

"I need those ashes. I need proof the book was destroyed."

"I'll mail them to you. Now go."

Stillwell snorted in disgust. "You're a witch

hunter. You really think she's going to want you around?"

Charlotte stuck her head around the hall entrance. "I already do."

"How did you do that?" Stillwell asked. "How did you destroy something that powerful?"

She shrugged. "I guess it listened to me. It had already picked me as its keeper, so why wouldn't it? Now seriously, get out of Walker's apartment or I will zap you again."

Stillwell left to the sound of Walker chuckling.

He locked the door as soon as his former boss was through it. "Charlotte Fenchurch, you are one amazing woman."

She yawned and leaned against the wall. "Thanks. For saving my life. And for defending me. I'm sorry you lost your job."

He shrugged as he walked toward her. "I'm not."

"But the FOL is all you've known."

"I heard the sheriff's hiring…"

"No." Charlotte's brows went up. "Please don't become the next deputy of the month."

"What is that all about anyway?"

"I'll explain tomorrow. Right now, I need to lie down before I fall down."

"Let me help." He scooped her into his arms, taking advantage of her closeness to kiss her forehead and fill his senses with her perfume.

She leaned into him and sighed out the weariest breath he'd ever heard. "I can walk," she whispered.

"I know." He couldn't imagine how exhausted she was after everything she'd been through. She'd been brave and strong and incredibly tough.

A new, surprising realization hit him. He wanted this woman beside him always.

He carried her back to the guest bedroom, nudged the door open with his elbow and walked into the room. Edgar Allan was curled up on one side of the bed, fast asleep.

"Hey, big man. Make room for your mama," Walker whispered.

He laid Charlotte down on the other side. She mumbled something, but her eyes stayed closed.

"Shh. Go to sleep. We'll talk in the morning." He pulled the quilt over her, turned out the light, and snuck across the hall to his bedroom.

He shut the door and leaned against it as the reality of everything that had just happened sank in.

Charlotte was right. The Fraternal Order of Light was all he'd ever known. It had been more than a job. The FOL had been his family. His home.

From this point on, he would be starting over. It was daunting. But he'd faced worse. And he wasn't going forward alone. He had Charlotte. Just the thought of her made this new road seem walkable.

He tugged his shirt off over his head, plans

already forming for tomorrow. He'd never really had a girlfriend. Or a reason to stay in one place for more than a month.

This was going to be fun.

CHARLOTTE WOKE up feeling like she'd been run over by a truck. She struggled to a sitting position, trying to unkink the stiffness in her body. Edgar Allan was nowhere around, but the smell of coffee told her Walker—and her cat—were probably in the kitchen.

She checked the time. Plenty early. Still in her pajamas, she stumbled out to see if her guess had been right.

It had been. Walker was setting the table. He looked entirely too chipper. Was he a morning person? Please don't let him be a morning person. That might be a deal breaker.

He greeted her with a smile. "Hey, you're up."

She nodded. She hadn't bothered to look in a mirror, but she had a pretty good idea of what she looked like, so she gave him points for not recoiling in horror. "Sort of."

He pulled out a chair. "You need coffee. And sustenance. Sit."

She trudged over and took the seat. Edgar Allan was scarfing something down. "You fed my cat?"

"Is that okay? I cleaned the litter box too. I've never done that before. It was…interesting."

"It was gross. You can say it." She rubbed her eyes. The smell of coffee got closer. She pulled her hands away to see Walker filling her cup.

"Yeah, well, it's not going on my list of most favorite things, but I like Eddie, so I'm okay with cleaning up after him."

"Eddie?" She dumped sugar into her coffee, followed by creamer. Where had that come from? She didn't remember seeing half-and-half in his fridge.

"We talked about it. Sort of. He thinks Edgar Allan is fine as a given name, but it's a little formal for every day."

She stared at Walker. "You talked to my cat? He talked to you? Were you a leopard when this—you know what? I need caffeine more than I need that story right now because without it, the story isn't going to make much sense anyway."

"I'll just say it's not talking so much as it's more of a feeling he gives off." Walker laughed and went to the counter. "I'll tell you all about it when you've had your coffee."

She took a few long sips of the coffee. It was good. Really good. She was already starting to feel more human.

Then Walker put a plate of pancakes and bacon

in front of her, along with a paper coffee cup full of maple syrup.

She thought that might be the moment she really fell in love. "You made pancakes?"

"No, sorry. These are from Chickadee's. I got takeout."

"You went to Chickadee's." Maybe being a morning person wasn't so bad. "Before I got up."

"Mm-hmm."

Okay, yes, she was in love. He'd gotten up early to get her breakfast. Pancakes and bacon, no less. "Will you marry me? I realize that's a bit hasty, but this feels like a situation I need to lock down."

He laughed, hard. "Maybe you should eat something before you make any big decisions. And drink the rest of that coffee."

She was too busy devouring a strip of bacon to answer.

He joined her with a plate for himself. "I guess you're going into work today?"

She nodded and drizzled syrup over her pancakes. "I'm on the schedule. Plus, Millie obviously won't be there, so someone has to open up." She sighed as she cut into the fluffy stack with her fork. "It's going to be nuts with her gone. No one will know why, I won't be able to explain it and—"

"You won't have to. It'll be handled."

She drank some coffee to wash the pancakes down. "What do you mean?"

"I mean the FOL doesn't leave threads untied. When you get to work this morning, you'll find it's not the mess you're expecting. If anyone asks, which they probably won't, just tell them Millie went to Canada to discover herself."

"Seriously?"

"Seriously."

"It would be nice if it was that easy." She ate some more pancakes. They were delicious and completely not on her diet. But today that seemed like the least of her concerns. "They'll have to hire a new head librarian. I really hope it's me, but if it's not, then I at least hope they find someone nicer than Millie."

"That wouldn't take much doing, would it?"

She smirked. "No, it wouldn't. Hey, you need to get your truck."

"I'll ride with you to work. Cool?"

"Cool." He was awfully happy for a man who'd just left his life behind him. She looked at him a little harder, trying to see if his eyes were hiding something. She couldn't tell. "You okay with all this?"

"Breakfast? I love breakfast."

She frowned. "You know what I mean. You're starting over. That's scary. Or at least it could be."

He shook his head slowly. "It's all good. Unless you suddenly decide you don't want to be friends anymore. I was kind of counting on having you around to help ease the transition."

She couldn't help but smile at that. "I'm not going anywhere." But he might be. She sat up. "Who paid for this place?"

"The FOL. But it's paid through the month, so I'm not about to be homeless."

"That's good. I was trying to figure out how we were going to make it work in my one bedroom."

He stared at her without saying anything for a long moment, a forkful of pancakes lifted toward his mouth, but froze. "You were…going to invite me to move in with you?"

"I didn't think you'd have anywhere else to go. And you're out of a job. Hard to rent a place without one." She ran the end of a bacon strip through the syrup on the plate. "You have to live somewhere and after what we've just been through, I think I know you pretty well."

He smiled. "That's incredibly sweet of you. Also generous and kind. I'm going to work on my housing situation today. I'll let you know how it turns out when you get home tonight. Unless you were planning on going back to your place?"

She sighed. "I've been trying not to think about that. I need to ask the sheriff if I can go back, which I'm sure I can, I just figured I'd better get the official word. It's such a mess."

"I said I would help and I will. I've literally got nothing better to do."

She laughed. "Okay, let me see how things go today." She got up. "I'd better get ready." Then she hesitated. "Hey, do you think I still get my wish? From Middian's, I mean? With the book destroyed, I wasn't sure."

"I'd say probably not. Was there something you were hoping for?"

She smiled. "Isn't everyone always hoping for something? It's no big deal."

But getting the job of head librarian would be nice. Even nicer would be keeping Walker here in Everlasting. Without a job or a place to live, that felt like a very unsettled outcome.

An hour later, they were pulling into the library's main parking lot. "I guess I could park in the back in Millie's old spot, seeing as how she won't be needing it anymore. Except her car is still in it."

"No, it's not. Like I said, the FOL cleans up after itself. Drive on around, you'll see. Plus my truck is still back there."

She headed around to drop him off so he could move his vehicle. Millie's old spot was empty, just like he'd said it would be.

"See?" He kissed her cheek before getting out of the car.

"You were right," she called after him. She pulled into the space with an odd mix of feelings. It was weird to park there, but she'd only have it until they sent a new head librarian, so she might as well enjoy it.

Walker was already in his truck when she got out of her car. He put down his window and leaned out. "I'll meet you at your place right after seven and help you clean up. Unless the sheriff tells you differently. Text me, okay?"

"I will. I hope you have a nice day."

"You too." He winked at her.

She gave him a little wave and watched him back out. The last few days seemed surreal, but Walker was most definitely flesh and blood. And he seemed to like her as much as she liked him. Which meant she had a boyfriend.

That word shouldn't make her giggle like a high schooler, but it kind of did. A boyfriend. She unlocked the back door and went in. A really hot boyfriend.

She flipped the lights on and started going through her opening routine. A few minutes later she heard knocking on the front door. She went to see who it was and found Norm Poole.

She unlocked the door. "What are you doing here? Today's your day off."

"I got a call from the head office telling me my schedule had been changed starting immediately. Apparently, I've been bumped up to full time until further notice."

Charlotte knew it wasn't the head office that had called him. "Are you good with that?"

"Sure. Could always use a little extra money."

"Great. Come on in. I'm happy to have the help." She liked Norm. He was easygoing, never complained, and knew his books.

He nodded as he entered. "Yep. I heard Millie ran off to Canada. Some middle-age crisis thing. Except she's kind of beyond middle-age." He laughed. "You just never know about people, do you?"

"No, you don't." Amazing how fast the story about Millie had spread. The FOL was obviously a powerful organization, but she'd be just fine if they never showed up in Everlasting again. She got Norm started on some reshelving, then went to collect the books that had been dropped off through the return slot overnight.

Thankfully, the only books in there were library books.

The phone rang promptly at nine. She answered, sort of hoping it was Walker checking in. "Everlasting Library, Charlotte Fenchurch speaking."

"Miss Fenchurch, this is Arnold Ruskin from the Maine Library Association. I'd like to talk to you about Mildred Merriweather."

Chapter Twenty-Two

Walker arrived at Charlotte's apartment later than he'd intended, but the day's events had taken more time than anticipated. He ran up the stairs, eager to tell her his news. He knocked on the apartment door, noticing the new lock.

"Come in!" she called out.

He opened the door. The mess was all still there, but he could tell she'd already made some progress in the kitchen. "How's it going?"

She rolled her eyes. "Slowly." She shook her head and looked around. "I have to be honest. I don't even want to be here. It feels…tainted."

He bit the inside of his cheek to keep from laughing out loud at the news he was about to share. "You should move."

"I'd love to. But I don't have the money." Suddenly her face lit up in a huge smile. "Although I will soon. Well, I'll have more money anyway. They offered me the job of head librarian! Can you believe it? That was going to be my wish if I got to make one and it came true anyway!"

"That's amazing. Congratulations!" He came around to meet her. "They're lucky to have you."

Her hands shot into the air and she let out a whoop. "I'm so excited. It's a raise and better hours and I get to hire the person to replace me. Plus Norm is going full time until my replacement is hired, and I like him a lot. You were right about the FOL tying up loose ends. Everyone seems to think Millie's gone off to find herself in Canada just like you said they would."

"Told you. I'm sure you'll soon hear something similar about Lola, too."

"I don't like Stillwell, but I'll give him credit for taking care of all that." She frowned. "What about the judge? I have to admit, I feel a little bad for him. He did some awful things, but it was in the name of love and that sort of makes me wish he'd had a better end."

Walker laughed. "As it just so happens, Stillwell caught him, the mouse version of him, and is taking him back to FOL headquarters to see if they can undo the spell. He thinks there's a pretty good chance they'll have him back in human form shortly."

"Will they let him come back to town?"

"Yes, so long as he signs a non-disclosure agreement and promises to behave himself. He'll still be under FOL scrutiny for the rest of his life, but that knowledge should be enough to keep him on the straight and narrow."

"How about that. I'm happy he's getting a second chance. Not sure I'll ever be able to have him in the library without giving him the side eye, though."

"Speaking of the library…" He pulled her into his arms, clasping his hands at the small of her back. "Head librarian, huh?"

She beamed. "Yep. I am so excited. It's a dream come true."

"You know, you really should move now. I mean, the head librarian needs to live somewhere more prestigious. Some place like that big white house on Maple that's for sale. You know the one with the three brick chimneys and that massive front porch?"

She narrowed her eyes. "The one with the black shutters and the red front door? That's the Timmons' place. I love that house. I've been through it every year on the tour of homes, but when I said I'm getting a raise, I meant about a twenty percent increase, not triple what I'm currently making. I still wouldn't be able to afford that castle."

He smiled. "So you don't want to move in there?"

She kept squinting at him. "You're acting weird. Yes, I'd love to move in there, but like I said, I can't afford it."

He shrugged. "It's off the market anyway."

"It is? I wonder who bought it."

He nodded. "I did. Today. Sad you don't want to live there with me, especially because that big backyard would be perfect for Eddie, but if that's how you feel—"

"What? Back up." She grabbed his arms, her eyes wide. "You bought the Timmons' house? How? You don't have a job."

He laughed. "No, I don't have a job, but I've worked for the FOL all my life. They've paid me handsomely. And I spent very little. I had the money. And I liked the house." He suddenly realized what a hasty decision that had been. "Crap. I should have asked you first. I was just assuming you'd like that place and it really does have a great backyard and—"

She kissed him, sending little sparks of pleasure up his spine.

He tightened his arms, tugging her closer and leaning into the embrace. He broke the kiss to trail more of them over her jaw and down her neck. "I've never kissed a head librarian before. Feels a little naughty, but I like it. Might even say it's been long *overdue*."

She giggled. "You're nuts." She pulled back to

look at him. "That's the other thing I was going to wish for. You, staying here in Everlasting. I'm so happy."

"Me, too."

She bit her bottom lip. "Is this going to work?"

"Living together? The place has two floors, six bedrooms, and a finished basement. I think there's enough space for the three of us."

"No, silly. I meant…us." She smoothed the front of his shirt, no longer making eye contact. "I'm a witch, not much of one admittedly, but I am what I am. And you're a witch hunter."

"*Retired* witch hunter. Who only ever hunted bad witches. You're a good witch." He grinned. "A very good witch. And now I'm just a regular old independently wealthy leopard shifter who dabbles in antiques."

She snorted. "You do present such an attractive case."

He took her hands in his and kissed them. "I adore you, Charlotte. Maybe we're headed into this a little fast, but so what? We'll figure it out as we go. And if you're okay with that, I am too." He cocked his head. "Are you okay with that?"

She nodded. "I am."

Then she leaned in. "You know what else I'd be okay with?"

He kissed the tip of her nose. "What?"

"Leaving this mess of an apartment for another day and going to get pizza."

He whirled her toward the door. "Remo's here we come."

She pulled his arm over her shoulders. "And then maybe afterward, we could take a walk out by the lighthouse. You know, they say it has a ghost. Oh, and supposedly, if you bury a penny in the dirt around it, your wish will come true. Then you could have one too."

He looked at her. "I can skip that part." He beamed at her, knowing his eyes were filled with the glow of his beast and his adoration for her. "All my wishes have already come true."

THE END

Newsletter

Want to be up to date on new books, new audiobooks & other fun stuff from me?

Sign-up for my NEWSLETTER.

No spam, just news (sales, freebies, releases, you know, all that jazz.)

If you loved the book and want to help the series grow, tell a friend about the book and take time to leave a review!

About the Author

Kristen Painter is a little obsessed with cats, books, chocolate, and shoes. It's a healthy mix. She loves to entertain her readers with interesting twists, entertaining stories and unforgettable characters. She currently writes the best-selling paranormal romance series, Nocturne Falls, and the cozy mystery spin off, the Jayne Frost mysteries. The former college English teacher can often be found all over social media where she loves to interact with readers:

Instagram

https://kristenpainter.com/

Other books by Kristen Painter

PARANORMAL ROMANCE

Nocturne Falls series:

The Vampire's Mail Order Bride

The Werewolf Meets His Match

The Gargoyle Gets His Girl

The Professor Woos The Witch

The Witch's Halloween Hero – short story

The Werewolf's Christmas Wish – short story

The Vampire's Fake Fiancée

The Vampire's Valentine Surprise – short story

The Shifter Romances The Writer

The Vampire's True Love Trials – short story

The Dragon Finds Forever

The Vampire's Accidental Wife

Can't get enough Nocturne Falls?

Try the Nocturne Falls Universe books.

New stories, new authors, same Nocturne Falls world!

Sin City Collectors series:

Queen of Hearts

Dead Man's Hand

Double or Nothing

Box set

Standalone Paranormal Romance:

Dark Kiss of the Reaper

Heart of Fire

Recipe for Magic

Miss Bramble and the Leviathan

COZY PARANORMAL MYSTERY

Miss Frost Solves A Cold Case – A Nocturne Falls
Mystery

Miss Frost Ices The Imp – A Nocturne Falls Mystery

Miss Frost Saves The Sandman – A Nocturne Falls
Mystery

More Everlasting...

COZY PARANORMAL MYSTERY ROMANCE NOVELS

The Happily Everlasting Series

Dead Man Talking
by Jana DeLeon

Once Hunted, Twice Shy
by Mandy M. Roth

Fooled Around and Spelled in Love
by Michelle M. Pillow

Witchful Thinking
by Kristen Painter

Visit Everlasting
https://welcometoeverlasting.com/

Dead Man Talking

by Jana DeLeon

Welcome to Everlasting, Maine, where there's no such thing as normal.

Meteorologist Zoe Parker put Everlasting in her rearview mirror as soon as she had her college degree in hand. But when Sapphire, her eccentric great-aunt, takes a tumble down the stairs in her lighthouse home, Zoe returns to the tiny fishing hamlet to look after her. Zoe has barely crossed the county line when strange things start happening with the weather, and she discovers Sapphire's fall was no accident. Someone is searching the lighthouse but Sapphire has no idea what they're looking for. Determined to ensure her aunt's ongoing safety, Zoe promises to expose the intruders, even though it means staying in Everlasting and confronting the past she thought she'd put behind her.

Dane Stanton never expected to see Zoe standing in the middle of her aunt's living room, and was even more unprepared for the flood of emotion he experiences when coming face to face with his old flame. Zoe is just as independent and determined as he remembered, and Dane knows she won't rest until Sapphire can return to the light-house in peace, so he offers to help her sort things out.

Armed with old legends, Sapphire's ten cats, and a talking ghost, Zoe has to reconcile her feelings for Dane and embrace her destiny before it's too late.

Once Hunted, Twice Shy

by Mandy M. Roth

Welcome to Everlasting, Maine, where there's no such thing as normal.

Wolf shifter Hugh Lupine simply wants to make it through the month and win the bet he has with his best friend. He's not looking to date anyone, or to solve a murder, but when a breath taking beauty runs him over (literally) he's left no choice but to take notice of the quirky, sassy newcomer. She'd be perfect if it wasn't for the fact she's the grand-daughter of the local supernatural hunter. Even if he can set aside his feelings about her family, Penelope is his complete opposite in all ways.

Penelope Messing wanted to get away from the harsh reminder that her boyfriend of two years dumped her. Several pints of ice cream and one plane ticket to Maine later, she's ready to forget her troubles. At least for a bit. When she arrives in the sleepy little fishing town of Everlasting, for a surprise visit with her grandfather, she soon learns that outrunning one problem can lead to a whole mess of others. She finds herself the prime suspect in a double homicide. She doesn't even kill spiders, let alone people, but local law enforcement has their eyes on her.

The secrets of Everlasting come to light and Penelope has to not only accept that things that go bump in the night are real, but apparently, she's destined for a man who sprouts fur and has a bizarre obsession with fish sticks. Can they clear Penelope's name and set aside their differences to find true love?

Fooled Around and Spelled in Love

by Michelle M. Pillow

Welcome to Everlasting, Maine, where there's no such thing as normal.

Anna Crawford is well aware her town is filled with supernaturals, but she isn't exactly willing to embrace her paranormal gifts. Her aunt says she's a witch-in-denial. All Anna wants is to live a quiet "normal" life and run her business, Witch's Brew Coffee Shop and Bakery. But everything is about to be turned upside down the moment Jackson Argent walks into her life.

Jackson isn't sure why he agreed to come back to his boyhood home of Everlasting. It's like a spell was cast and he couldn't say no. Covering the Cranberry Festival isn't exactly the hard-hitting news this reporter is used to. But when a local death is ruled an accident, and the police aren't interested in investigating, he takes it upon himself to get to the bottom of the mystery. To do that, he'll need to enlist the help of the beautiful coffee shop owner.

It soon becomes apparent things are not what they seem and more than coffee is brewing in Everlasting.

Witchful Thinking

by Kristen Painter

Welcome to Everlasting, Maine, where there's no such thing as normal.

Charlotte Fenchurch knows that, which is why she's not that surprised when a very special book of magic falls into her hands at the library where she works. As a fledgling witch, owning her own grimoire is a dream come true. But there's something…mysterious about the book she just can't figure out.

Leopard shifter Walker Black knows what's odd about the book. It's full of black magic and so dangerous that it could destroy the world. Good thing the Fraternal Order of Light has sent him to Everlasting to recover it and put it into safe storage.

If he has to, he'll even take the witch who owns it into custody.

That is until he meets Charlotte and realizes she's not out to watch the world burn. She's sweet and kind and wonderful. Suddenly protecting her is all he wants to do. Well, that and kiss her some more. But dark forces seem determined to get their hands on the book, making Charlotte their target, and Walker worries that he won't be able to protect her from them – or the organization he works for.

Can Walker and Charlotte survive the onslaught of danger? Or is that just witchful thinking?

Visit Everlasting

https://welcometoeverlasting.com/

89110671R00170

Made in the USA
Middletown, DE
13 September 2018